Cowboy, Kiss Me at Christmas
Cowboy Homecoming
Book 5

Genevieve Turner

1

When Sasha had said she dreamed of snow for Christmas, this wasn't what she meant.

In books, snow for Christmas was cute, cozy. A reason to stay in by the fire or go out and make snowmen. In her beloved romances, it guaranteed forced proximity. That was her favorite—two people stuck in a charming cabin with no choice but to fall for each other. The snow in those stories was great because then people were going to fall in love.

That was what she'd wanted when she wished for snow. A chance to cozy up with the man meant for her. Just the two of them, falling in love, as delicate flakes blanketed the outside world.

This snow was nothing like that. It was angry, battering, blinding. This was an actual blizzard, which wasn't supposed to happen in the Southern California mountains. It definitely wasn't supposed to happen when she was driving up winding roads with sheer drop-offs to visit her friend Pippa for Christmas.

"Come celebrate with us," Pippa had said. "We've got goats. And chickens. And you can't be alone at Christmas."

Of course Sasha could be alone at Christmas. She'd been alone last Christmas and the one before that. Flying home to Florida was too expensive. And video calls somehow made the loneliness worse, seeing her entire family gathered on one side of a screen and Sasha all by herself on the other.

Pippa had meant well with the invitation, and Sasha had been excited at first. Pippa had found a hot cowboy up there, and Lulu had found a hot mechanic—maybe there'd be someone for Sasha. Another hot cowboy or mechanic just waiting to make all her dreams come true. The man who'd been waiting his entire life for her.

She was so lonely. That was probably the only problem with reading so many romances. She immersed herself in descriptions of the purest, most emotional love, but once she put the book down, she was all alone. Those moments when she looked around her room, heart bursting but no one to share it with, hurt worse than the breakup scenes in her romances.

Pippa had tried to set Sasha up with her cousin, but it hadn't worked out. Ansel had been very nice... but he was also in love with someone else. Terribly, hopelessly in love, which had plucked right at Sasha's tender heartstrings. She wanted to be that helplessly in love with someone.

But she wasn't. Ansel had needed advice on how to turn his situation around, and Sasha had happily provided it. He'd done what she'd suggested, and now the lucky girl was as in love with him as he was with her.

It was a beautiful story, and Sasha had been glad to help, but it was bittersweet for her too. All that romance reading, and she could help everyone but herself.

Sasha shook off her self-pity and focused harder on the road. If she didn't, she'd be something much worse than alone this Christmas—she'd be dead.

Hunched over the steering wheel, she let the car idle forward through the swirl of white, foot hovering over the brake pedal, searching for any sign of the road.

"I'm gonna die," she muttered. "I'm gonna die."

Her mind started to wander again. If this were a romance novel, she wouldn't die. Instead, she'd... She'd plant the car in a snowbank. Gently, so she wasn't hurt. Not badly at least. Maybe just a touch of blood. But it would seem hopeless. Tears would freeze to her cheeks. She'd write a goodbye note to her friends and family, to be found with her body.

She might think about her regrets. About how she'd never had a chance to know the love of a good man. And how terrible it was that she was dying a virgin. She could be a virgin again, in this fantasy.

She'd feel her life slipping away.

But then... In the distance... What was that?

A man.

A tow truck driver. Wait, no, no, not in this fantasy, not this time. Something more... Something different...

She pursed her lips and made her imaginings take shape.

A cowboy. Riding a horse. Magically appearing through the drifts. Just as a dark, dreamless sleep was about to take her. Just as she was about to surrender to the deadly cold.

"Wake up." He'd slap her cheeks, just enough to rouse her. An impression of dark eyes, shadowed jaw under his hat. Voice like sin. He'd be gruff but tender. Tender only with *her*. The woman he'd been waiting his entire life for. "Don't you die on me—"

3

Sasha jerked her focus back to the road. This was no time to indulge in her fantasies. Her mother had always said Sasha was going to get hit by a bus with her daydreaming. It would be way too ironic to crash the car while she was dreaming up a scenario where she crashed the car. And there was definitely no cowboy out riding in this, ready to rescue her.

The only people out here in this storm had no concern for their own well-being. And she supposed that included her.

She steered into a wickedly tight turn, just barely making out the centerline through the white noise of the snow. If she lost that line even for a moment—

The car kept moving forward even though she had the wheel cranked all the way to the right.

Sliding, we're sliding.

A panicky loop started in her brain. What to do? She smashed on the brakes instinctively.

Nothing happened. She smashed again, her palms going slick on the wheel. Her leg was shaking.

No, wait, she wasn't supposed to hit the brakes. Something about making the car slide more? She'd read it in a book somewhere, a romantic suspense where the heroine had been left for dead in Alaska and she had to find her way back to civilization. Part of that was figuring out how to drive on the ice, and the hero was wounded, so she had to get him to a doctor and he couldn't help her with the driving.

God, how did she remember all that and not how to drive on ice?

The car kept sliding. Turning the wheel—she was supposed to do that—it suddenly came to her. But she was already turning the wheel—

4

With a neck-snapping thump, the car landed in the massive wall of snow on the side of the road.

Sasha blinked the stars out of her eyes and tried to catch her breath. Her neck was blazing with pain, her lungs were smashed from the seat belt, and nausea was rising fast and hard in her belly.

That was not a gentle landing. She was actually *hurt*.

After several long moments and many deep breaths, she got ahold of herself. The stars disappeared, although the aches hung around. So did the sour feeling in her stomach.

The car had died on its own somehow. Maybe the engine was broken. Or the snow had done it. She didn't know and her brain hurt too much to think about for too long.

It took several shoves to get the car door open. Sasha spilled out on shaky legs, the snow practically attacking her. Immediately she started shivering.

The car was sunk into the snowbank, about three feet of the hood disappearing into it. She'd never be able to get it out.

The vision of her curling up, eyes fluttering shut, cheeks blue, surrendering to the cold, flashed through her mind. It looked like at least one part of her little daydream was going to come true—the hideous-death part. The worst part.

She started to shiver, her body shaking violently. Her pink chenille sweater with mint-green Christmas trees was cute and fuzzy but not that warm. And she was already wearing her heaviest jacket.

When she opened the trunk and found the blanket she'd packed, she heaved a sigh of relief. It was a blanket Pippa had given her—Pippa had found it in the rubble of her collapsed house (that was a long, awful story), and it was miraculously intact. The blanket was crocheted in shades of purple and blue and looked exactly like one Sasha remembered her grandma having on her couch. Sasha had loved that blanket, which had always smelled like her grandma's love to her.

Grandma had passed after Sasha had moved out to California, and she hadn't had the money to make it back for the funeral. When she'd asked her mom about the blanket, Mom hadn't known anything about it. The blanket was probably long gone into some cousin's house, or worse, into a dumpster.

When Sasha had exclaimed in surprise at seeing the almost-identical blanket on Pippa's bed, Pippa had given it to her. Which was typical Pippa, who would have given it to Sasha even if they weren't best friends.

Sasha had kept the blanket with her ever since, even putting it in her car when she left the house. She couldn't explain it, but she felt better when she knew the blanket was near. And it was practically the perfect blanket, not too hot or too cold no matter what the weather was. She could pull it over her anytime and feel better.

Pulling it over her shoulders right now instantly made her feel warmer. The blanket wasn't any heavier than her jacket, but she immediately stopped shivering.

The blanket couldn't stop the storm though. The snow blew into her face and hair, freezing any exposed patch of skin. Her cheeks were already numb.

Sasha considered her options. Staying with the car didn't seem safe. If another car came along and hit it, she'd be toast. And her head didn't feel so good. She needed to find shelter and some help. Somewhere.

But walking out into a snowstorm wasn't smart either. She wasn't likely to lose the road, and there were houses somewhere along here, but... But she was scared. She didn't want to die out here.

Honestly, who died at Christmas in a blizzard? That was only supposed to happen in Western historicals, the heroine wandering the prairie, the hero desperate to find her, finally realizing just how much he loved her. But it would be too late...

And again, she needed to stop doing that. Sasha shook her head, and pain rattled through her skull. *Please don't let me have a brain injury.* There had to be shelter around here somewhere. If she called 911, someone had to come.

But when she looked at her phone, there was no signal. There hadn't been for at least twenty minutes.

Panic bubbled in her chest, but she forced herself to think. This was Southern California; there was no way she could die in a blizzard.

Holding the blanket tight around her, she began to creep along the side of the road, or at least what should have been the side of the road. She didn't want to get hit by a car coming too fast in this mess.

Every few minutes she wrestled her phone out of the blanket and checked for a signal. Nothing. And each time she did it, more cold crept in under the blanket and she couldn't seem to drive it out. Her toes were so numb they crackled. Her cheeks burned with the wind and snow. She blinked furiously to clear her lashes, but it wasn't enough.

Frozen, blinded, she stumbled on.

Every breath was a knife in her lungs. It felt like her throat was shredding from the cold.

She tripped over something in the road, or maybe her legs just weren't working anymore. It was hard to tell. Her body felt fuzzy where it wasn't searingly cold, as if it were dissolving into the snow.

Get up. But it was so hard. She was on her hands and knees, gravel biting into her palms. There wasn't any more strength in her. She couldn't rise.

Dimly, she realized she wasn't shivering anymore. That was...

Couldn't remember what it was. So tired. If she closed her eyes... That was bad. She remembered that.

She also couldn't help it. She didn't even have the strength to keep her eyes open.

As she slipped into the welcoming darkness, her last thought was *Even the tow truck driver would be good about now.*

This place was warm. And it smelled good.

Sasha groaned happily as she rolled over. The mattress was hard as a rock, but oh, she was so *warm*.

This was the warmest she'd ever been. Not hot, not at all, but like being wrapped in the best hug ever. And it smelled like her grandma's house. And baking. It smelled like home and was warm like love.

Her hand connected with something soft, furry. She pet it, nuzzling her hand into the nap. Oh, this was warm too. A warm, fuzzy—

Her face was bathed in wet warmth, something rough and slinky running over it.

A tongue. Something was licking her. Something big.

She screamed and threw herself backward. Every ache in her body came alive then, and there were a lot.

She screamed again.

The creature bawled. Loud and long and pitiful.

Sasha took a shaky breath and then another. Her

vision was blurry and her head was pounding. The thing yelling at her was a big brown lump, lying on the floor with her.

Why was she on the floor with this... thing? And there was heat coming from somewhere. She felt it on the left side of her face, so hot now it was uncomfortable.

The brown fuzzy thing yelled again.

Sasha rubbed her eyes. Slowly the room came into focus. It was some kind of cabin, a single room with one chair and a table, some cabinets, and a potbellied stove that was providing the heat. She was lying on a mattress on the floor, her blanket wrapped around her.

At her feet was the fuzzy brown thing.

It was a baby *calf.*

Her heart skipped a beat. It was the cutest thing ever. Big brown eyes, wet nose, and ears a size too large for its head. Its tongue slithered out to lick its own nose.

"Eww." Sasha wiped her face with the blanket, wishing she had some tissues. "You licked me! That was way grosser than it sounded in that Minotaur romance."

The calf simply blinked at her. It was wrapped in a blanket too. It was on the floor instead of the mattress but close enough to the stove to share in its warmth.

"How did you get here?" She rubbed the calf's head, clutching the blanket to her chest with her other hand. It was the only familiar thing she had, and she found she couldn't let go of it. "How did *I* get here?"

The calf didn't answer. Her head pounded like she was in the middle of the worst hangover of her life. And her clothes...

Sasha peeked under the blanket. These weren't her clothes! Someone had undressed her, and she was pretty sure it wasn't the calf. She had on an oversized T-shirt and some gray sweatpants. The drawstring at the waist was cinched tight, the better to stay on her.

Maybe she'd been rescued by a mountain man. A burly, bearded hermit who thought he had no heart, rejecting all human comfort. But despite his wounds, he couldn't leave her to die.

Underneath his crusty exterior would be a soft heart, ready to love again when the right woman came along. Which might be her. Maybe he'd felt a strange pull as he rescued her, his heart reacting in an odd way. But deep inside, he knew—

The calf licked her again, dissolving that fantasy.

"Are you hungry?" She looked around, but she didn't see a bottle. Or anything to eat or drink at all.

Maybe this was an animal barn. It was a little depressing that her rescuer would put her in a barn. But maybe it was the warmest place he had. Certainly it was warmer than out in the snow.

"Is he coming back?" she asked the calf.

Or maybe her rescuer was a woman. A bit rude of Sasha to assume it was a mountain man. Or a cowboy. Or a tow truck driver.

Although they did have cows. So they were a cow *something*. Cowperson. Yeah, that worked.

She should see if her phone was around here somewhere. Strangely, she wasn't too worried about her mysterious rescuer. If they were planning on robbing or torturing or even murdering her, they wouldn't have put her in with this adorable calf.

Unless it was a veal calf.

Sasha gasped and clasped her throat. "Oh my goodness. You poor baby. I'm going to get us both out of here."

Except that standing up proved to be more difficult than

usual. Impossible, actually. It turned out that almost freezing to death was really bad for a person even if they survived.

Sasha could get to her hands and knees, but trying to stand made her head spin like it was in a washing machine. Her stomach spun too. Her legs were so weak they collapsed whenever she put weight on them.

She'd have to crawl around the room to get anywhere. And as soon as she moved away from the stove and her warm nest, she started shivering again. And the calf would cry when she got more than a foot away.

"This is not good," she muttered. But she had to find her phone, see where she was. And could call 911 or AAA or whoever came to rescue people from mountain men's veal barns. "I guess I'll crawl then."

She started for the cabinets, hoping to be able to climb up to open one. Maybe her clothes and phone were in there. But it was so far, so much farther than it looked. She was panting before she'd even gotten a few feet, her vision swimming in and out of focus.

"This was a bad choice," she moaned.

"You think?"

A pair of boots came into her vision. Worn, covered in dust, the kind of boots that had seen a lot of hard work. And the voice...

She looked up. Oh boy, he was far away. She could see a cowboy hat, broad shoulders, fur around his neck and—

Sasha toppled over, her spinning head too much for her poor balance.

"Damn."

She was scooped up in strong arms, too weak to even try to protest. She was held firmly against a broad chest, carried as if she weighed nothing. The man set her gently back on the mattress, tucking the blanket around her. The calf mooed a happy welcome.

"Stay there," he ordered.

Oh, he sounded... grim and mean. Just like he was supposed to in a romance novel, except it wasn't as exciting as it should have been. It was kind of scary even though he'd been careful when he'd touched her.

"Thank you for rescuing me," she said weakly.

He grunted. His back was to her as he rummaged in one of the cabinets. It turned out the fur around his neck was actually a sheepskin collar. He looked very warm.

She shivered again even though the stove was nice and toasty and her blanket kept her warm. "How did you find me?"

"Why were you out on the road?" He set a gallon jug on the table, then pulled down a massive red rubber nipple.

Whoa. That was quite the bottle.

"I was driving up to Cabrillo," she said, still staring at the nipple. Where did he even find one that size? "My friend is there. My car slid off the road, and I didn't have a signal— Where's my phone?"

He fished something out of his pocket and tossed it to her. It bounced off the blanket and almost into the calf.

Sasha glared at his back as she reached over to grab it. Really, he could have handed it to her. This grumpy act wasn't sexy at all—it was just rude. In the books, her heart would be pounding with suppressed lust. Instead, all she felt was sour resentment.

"Thanks," she said sarcastically.

That got him to turn around. She got an impression of dark eyes, strong brows, a rugged jaw. His age was hard to determine, but maybe thirtyish? Her heart did not immediately react to his features.

Again, this was not at all how it would have gone down in a romance. How sad that she'd finally been rescued for the first time in her life and it was turning out like the rest of her life—disappointing.

"You shouldn't have gotten out of the car."

Well, wasn't he judgy. "I was looking for shelter."

"There was none."

"I didn't know that." She pushed up to her elbow, then immediately regretted it when her stomach flipped over. Slowly she lay back down and closed her eyes. "I think I need a doctor."

"You do." His voice was close now.

When she opened her eyes, he was giving the calf the bottle. The calf drank it up gratefully, wide eyes framed by thick lashes. Its throat worked in long swallows. Really, it was the most adorable thing.

"Does he have a name?" she asked.

"She." His tone was even gruffer. "No, not yet."

"Do *you* have a name?"

"Max."

No last name, huh? "I'm Sasha." She considered putting her hand out to shake, but he didn't seem like he wanted to and she wasn't quite feeling steady enough to try it.

"You shouldn't have been driving in that."

"I didn't know there was going to be a blizzard. That kind of snow isn't supposed to happen here."

"It is a thousand-year storm," he admitted grudgingly.

"What were you doing out in it? Because you had to be out there to find me."

"I found you at the end of the driveway." His mouth compressed. "I had to get something, but I couldn't get out."

It must have been something important if he'd go out in

13

a blizzard. And then he'd found her, half-dead, and he couldn't finish his trip.

"I'm sorry," she said. "I'm feeling better. You could go get it now."

He shook his head. "Nothing's getting in or out for a few days. A deep freeze is coming too."

Days? Sasha looked at her phone. If she had a signal, she could call someone, anyone, to get her out of here. But there was only a big, fat No Service where her bars should have been.

Pippa must be losing her mind. Sasha would be if their roles were switched. She had to get a message to her friend somehow. Too bad carrier pigeons weren't around anymore. That seemed like the only thing that would work with everything else being down.

That made her think about pigeons in books. She didn't think she'd ever read a romance with pigeons. Breeding pigeons used to be really popular—why weren't they ever in historical romances? If someone wrote one, she'd definitely read a romance with a heroine who raised pigeons.

Wait, she was supposed to be solving her problems here, not thinking about pigeons.

"Do you normally have service out here?"

He was pulling the bottle out of the calf's mouth. The calf blinked sleepily. "No."

"How do you survive?"

His mouth twitched like he might smile, then he turned his shoulder in so she couldn't see his face. "I couldn't say."

Well, he wasn't entirely humorless. Maybe.

All right. Time to take stock of where she was. She was alive and not going to die by the side of the road in a blizzard. In Southern California. If she had, she'd be the first person ever to do it, which would have been really embarrassing had she been alive to see the news stories.

She had her phone, but it had no service. She needed a doctor according to Max, and judging by how she felt, he was probably right. But a deep freeze was coming. So no doctor for her.

At least she was warm. And in a cow barn.

Actually— "Why did you put me in the barn?"

He looked around the room as he rose. "This isn't a barn —it's my house. And right here by the stove is the warmest place on the property. You both needed it."

Oh dear, she'd really offended him. But there was a freaking calf sitting across from her, and where did cows go except in a barn?

"Sorry," she mumbled. "Why does she need the warmth? Did she land her car into a snowbank too?"

He went still, the nipple on the bottle half screwed off. "Her mama is sick. Couldn't nurse her." His voice was strained.

Sasha grabbed for her heart. "Oh my God. I'm so sorry. How awful. The poor little thing." She gave the calf several long pets and some ear scritches to let her know she'd be okay and she was loved. "Will the mom be okay?"

"Can't tell yet."

The calf sighed and put her head on Sasha's knee, closing her eyes. It was the most tenderly adorable thing Sasha had ever seen. In that moment, her heart tumbled hard into love with the little thing.

"Will *she* be okay?" Sasha asked in a quiet voice, afraid of the answer.

"Maybe." He was quiet too.

Sasha ran her hand over the soft head, up the fuzzy ears.

So precious. Her heart was bursting. "She needs a name." She looked up at Max. "What's her mom's name?"

"Petunia. The calf looks just like her."

It was a lovely name. And while the calf didn't quite look like a flower, she made Sasha *think* of flowers. Of cows grazing in an endless meadow, the sun shining down, fluffy clouds floating by.

"What about Pansy? She could be a Pansy."

"Sure." Max didn't sound too enthused though. Maybe because he thought she might not make it.

A fierce swell of protectiveness rose in Sasha. There was no way she'd let anything happen to Pansy. Sasha had lived thanks to Max rescuing her, and now Pansy was going to live thanks to Sasha rescuing her.

If only she knew something about taking care of calves. "When does she need her next bottle? Do we even have any milk? Do I have to burp her?"

Max blinked slowly. His features were starting to come into focus. Dark skin, lines around his eyes from the sun. Strong brows, a prominent nose. Not anything to make Sasha look twice if she saw him on the street. Except he had a lower lip that was at odds with the rest of his features. Plush, made for sucking and nibbling on.

And whoops, there went her imagination! She'd definitely read too many books, because she wasn't going to be kissing this guy. As soon as the snow was melted, she was gone. And once Pansy was well enough to leave the house and go live with her mom and her cow friends.

"*We?*" he asked. "You're going to give her a bottle? And burp her?"

Embarrassed heat flooded Sasha's face. "I was only trying to help," she said stiffly. "You rescued me, so... I owe you. I'll be here anyway, so I might as well do something."

Max studied her for a long moment from dark eyes. Something stirred in Sasha. Not attraction since she wasn't attracted to him, but something kind of odd. Restless.

Probably just because he was staring at her like she had something on her face. Anyone would feel weird and squirmy.

Strange how she'd fallen into the perfect romance story scene, but it wasn't anything like she'd imagined. Maybe it was the baby cow. Maybe it was Max's curt attitude. Maybe it was how she was feeling, sick and banged up. Turned out that being dug out of a snowbank, close to death, kind of sucked.

"I guess you can help," he said after a while. "She gets colostrum right now. I'll get more from the freezer in the shop. Power's out, but I've got the generator running. Petunia's down, so the baby can't nurse. I can milk her out some, but she needs to get up, or..."

Sasha held her breath as she waited for him to finish that. When he didn't, she knew what he was leaving out—the cow would die.

"What's wrong with Petunia?"

"Milk fever," he said, as if that explained anything. "I gave her some calcium by IV, but she probably needs more. That's why I was going out. To get some."

And Sasha had ruined it by collapsing in his driveway. Poor Petunia might die and leave Pansy an orphan because Sasha had crashed in a storm. Because she'd been fantasizing about being rescued.

Well, this experience had killed that fantasy for her.

"I guess you can't just give her calcium pills or something." Sasha swallowed hard, but the guilt remained. "It's my fault, isn't it? That you couldn't go get it?"

17

"It's not," he said gruffly. "The roads would have been impassible no matter what. Just a bad time to be born."

"But it's Christmas!" Sasha wasn't sure why she'd said that. Yes, it was Christmas and normally a great time for a sweet baby calf to come into the world, but this Christmas was the worst, it was true. "Normally it'd be sweet. Actually, maybe we should call her Holly." Sasha's eyes went wide. "No, wait—Poinsettia!" She smacked herself in the forehead, then winced. Her headache practically clanged against her skull when she did that. "I can't believe I didn't think of that. Yes, she has to be Poinsettia."

Max wasn't at all excited by the calf's new name. "Poinsettia is toxic." He sighed. "I've got to go check on the horses. Are you all right? Do you need anything?"

Sasha took stock. Her vision was pretty much normal. Her head and her body still ached, but she wasn't shivering anymore. She wasn't going to risk standing up, but sitting didn't make her dizzy. That was good progress.

"I've never almost frozen to death," she admitted. "I feel like I'm getting better, but do you think I might need something else?"

"I've never almost frozen to death either. Scared the crap out of me when I found you." His gruff voice went even more gravelly. "Figured getting you warm was the best thing to do."

"Thank you." She suddenly felt shy, probably because he was clearly uncomfortable telling her that.

Oh, and he'd had to undress her! Sasha held in a gasp. No wonder he was embarrassed. Heat flooded her own face. What underwear was she wearing? She hadn't even thought about it when she'd put panties on this morning. And weren't you supposed to think about that—everyone seeing your underwear if you got in an accident?

She'd have to check once she had some privacy. Not that she had anything to change into.

"It wasn't..." Max lifted one shoulder. "If you don't need anything, I've got to do chores."

"I'm fine." Sasha sounded wildly cheery when she'd meant to only be upbeat. "I'll just follow Poinsettia's lead and take a nap. Sleep heals, you know."

He made a strangled noise that might have been a laugh. And then he was gone.

Sasha collapsed back into her blanket. The familiar smell surrounded her, home and grandma's hugs. She was warm and surprisingly cozy. Poinsettia made a sleepy noise and snuggled closer.

This was the strangest rescue she could ever have imagined.

2

Max Torres never cried.

Except apparently when his best milk cow was sick, when he'd rescued a half-frozen woman from the end of his drive, and when it was only two days from a Christmas he'd thought he'd be spending alone.

He never spent Christmas alone, not with *his* family. Not only was it huge, but Christmas was a monthlong event, starting with Las Posadas and ending with Three Kings' Day. Christmas was a season, not just a day.

But this actual Christmas Day, when he should have been making tamales with his aunts and uncles and trying to stay awake through midnight mass and listen to his younger cousins tell tales about their wild nights while his older, married cousins shook their heads, this Christmas he'd be trying to keep a cow and a woman alive instead of celebrating with his family.

When Sasha had asked him about Petunia, then insisted her calf would live and needed a name, he could hardly take it. He'd had to leave before he embarrassed himself.

Here in the barn, rubbing Petunia's neck, he could let

all the awfulness of the day simply wash over him without worrying about holding himself together. The day had been hellish from the first. Petunia had gone into labor too soon and then gone too long. Once the calf had come, the crisis wasn't over—she'd come down with milk fever, and even with the extra calcium, she wasn't getting up.

A downer cow didn't have much chance, and there wasn't anything more Max could do for her. It tore him up inside.

And then the storm had come up out of nowhere, inches of snow falling in minutes. There'd been no time to properly attend to the calf, not when he had a dozen horses to bring in. He trained performance cow horses, and they had to be first priority. But there was also Mopsy, his other milk cow, her calf, and the herd of Angus steers he kept to train his horses on to all bring in.

Mopsy and Petunia were in the barn with the horses, all the doors and windows shut up tight and snug. The other cattle had had to go in the covered arena since there wasn't a barn big enough to put them. They'd be making a complete disaster of the footing in there—so advanced it wasn't even dirt—but at least they weren't freezing to death.

Once the other animals were safely put up, Max had gone out to grab whatever calcium IV he could find, planning on hitting up every vet he knew in a fifty-mile radius.

And then he'd gotten to the end of the driveway, swinging open the gate, when he'd seen the snow-covered bundle on the shoulder. At first he hadn't thought anything of it, looking once, then back to the road. The snow was coming down like a fury, and he could barely see where he was supposed to be going.

Then a flash of purple had caught his eye. A bit of

fabric waving wildly from under a snowbank. Like it was trying to get his attention.

When he'd dug out some of the snow and seen her there, cold and frozen and lifeless, his heart had stopped. He'd pulled her out as fast as he could and still worried it was too late. There was so much snow on her she must have been out there a while. It was a miracle she was alive, what with that thin jacket she had on. Somehow that blanket had been the thing to save her, keeping her warm and grabbing his attention.

He knew he had to get her back to warmth and shelter, or else Sasha—the soft sigh of her name suited her—wasn't going to make it. Back to the house he'd gone, rubbing feeling back into her limbs, changing her cold, wet clothes, and putting her right next to the fire. She hadn't woken up then, but she was at least breathing.

The snow had kept coming the entire time, smothering his driveway and cutting off any chance he had of getting out. So there was no calcium for Petunia. She'd have to recover all on her own. At least there was some colostrum to give the new calf. Petunia might be in trouble, but hopefully her calf would pull through. He'd just have to hope the roads cleared sooner than he expected.

If that happened, it would help with the Sasha problem too. She seemed fine now, but when he'd found her, she'd been completely unresponsive and ice-cold. His heart froze at the memory, at how terrified he'd been for her. And all he could do was put her by the stove and pray it was enough. She needed a doctor, probably even a hospital, but there was no way he could get her to them.

Aside from getting her warm and dry, he hadn't known what to do. Beyond staring at her and feeling helpless, which he'd hated. So he'd left her by the stove and gone to fix the calf a bottle since it had started bawling.

Finding her awake had shocked the heck out of him. A good shock. And yet she still looked bad. Pale and weak with an unfocused gaze. Bad enough to keep him worried.

He hadn't expected this Christmas to be good since he wasn't going to be able to go home anyway what with Petunia being down. But he wasn't planning on it being this bad either.

He ran a hand over his face. At least he'd found Sasha in time. Funnily enough, his baby nephew—although at fifteen was that still a baby?—Leon, had told him just last week about how Leon was in love with a girl from his math class and sometimes fantasized about her being in trouble, him saving her, and her falling for him in gratitude.

Max had suggested that Leon simply talk to the girl instead and maybe spend math actually learning something. Leon hadn't been impressed with that advice, but maybe if he thought about it some, he'd realize Max was right.

Certainly when Max saw his nephew next, he could tell the kid that rescuing a woman from certain death wasn't anything to seek out. Mostly it was terrifying, the kind of thing that Max never wanted to experience again. He wasn't thinking about kissing Sasha when he pulled her, cold and lifeless, out of the snow.

He wasn't even thinking about it when she'd woken up. She was too fragile, too pale. It made the worry kick into high gear again.

He gave Petunia one last pat. She blinked at him as she chewed her cud, her serenity calming him. Even sick, she radiated peace and calm. There was nothing better than a milk cow to remind you to chill out.

"Get better," he said. "Your baby needs you."

She sighed heavily, but she showed no signs of wanting to get up.

One last circuit of the barn convinced him that everyone was doing fine and weathering the cold. Which meant he had to go back into the house now.

He turned up his collar before walking out into the cold, tucking his shoulders up to his ears. It was the kind of cold that punched him in the gut, sliced into the skin of his face. The kind of cold that wasn't supposed to happen here.

The skeleton of the new house sat empty and ghostly, the bare frame weighted with snow. When he'd moved out here, the horses had been his first priority. That meant the barn, the turnouts, and the arena had been built first. His house had to wait. He'd finally been able to start building on it, but it had been slow going. Which he hadn't cared about because the tack shed he'd refitted as a house suited him just fine.

It wouldn't do with two people in it though. Way too small for that. But he and Sasha'd have to make do.

He tramped up the front steps, kicking off some of the snow as he did. He scraped off as much mud and snow from his boots as he could, then opened the door and walked in.

The heat hit him first. It wrapped all around him, driving out the cold. His limbs loosened, his body no longer trying to lock in whatever heat it could. There was more than enough to go around here.

Then the scent of the bread he had going in the oven of the stove. Yeasty and rich, it made his stomach rumble.

Finally Sasha. Her big eyes blinked up at him from her nest of blankets, her color looking better than it had. Her hair was different somehow, falling around her shoulders. Her mouth was pink and lush and—

Aw *hell*. She was *pretty*. More than pretty, if she started

24

feeling any better, she'd be downright gorgeous. When he'd carried her in, she'd looked more like an icicle than anything else. And when he'd rubbed down her limbs, he'd only been thinking of reviving her.

If he rubbed her down now, he definitely would be thinking of other things. Like kissing her.

Maybe Leon had been onto something with his rescue fantasies.

She sat up, bracing herself on her elbow. "Is something wrong? What happened?"

"No." He started to toe off his boots, determined to think about anything but how pretty she was. "Why?"

"You were glaring at me like I'd done something." She shivered theatrically. "I thought you were going to call me into your office or something."

Jesus. She really couldn't say things like that. It messed with his mind. But then, his reaction to her was his own problem. Here she was, hurt and alone and lost, and he was scowling at her and being a perv.

"No office," he said shortly. "Everything's fine. At least not any worse than it was five minutes ago."

She laughed softly. "We've all had a pretty bad day, haven't we?" She ruffled the top of Poinsettia's head, including the calf in that. The gesture touched him more than it should have. Out of all the women he could have pulled out of a snowbank, he'd grabbed the pretty one who would love on his calf.

"The bread's almost done. And I brought in some soup to warm up too. Sorry, I don't have anything else."

With just himself to feed, he didn't have much in the way of groceries. Most of what he cooked was way too much for one person. Might as well only make one or two meals, make them last a few days or freeze the rest. Yeah, he got sick of a meal after two or three days of it, but that was how things went.

"That's it." Her nostrils flared in appreciation. "You're baking bread. That's what smells so good." She was smiling but had lain back into the blanket, tucking it under her chin. The purple of it made her dark hair stand out. She must still feel pretty bad if she couldn't sit up for long. But at least she was awake.

"I've got albóndigas soup too." He dumped the soup from a container into a pot and set it on the stove.

"I can't believe you make your own bread." Sasha frowned as she looked around the room. "It's... it's just you here, yes?"

"Me and the horses and the cows." He stirred the soup, then looked over his shoulder at her. "I train horses."

"You're a cowboy."

He smiled down at the soup. "I don't own enough cows for that."

"You own more cows than anyone else I know." She was cuddling Poinsettia again—he could tell from her tone. "I've never been this close to one in my entire life. How many do you have?"

"Two milk cows." He cleared his throat, wouldn't let himself think too much on Petunia. "The three calves. And about forty steers I use for training the horses."

"*Forty* cows? Yes, you're definitely a cowboy then."

There was something in the way she said it that trailed over his skin, leaving a wash of heat. He ignored it because she hadn't meant to do it.

He grabbed some kitchen towels, wrapped his hands, and pulled the bread out of the oven. The scent filled the small room.

"Oh my God." Sasha practically moaned that. "It smells so good."

Again, he ignored his reaction to her tone. Or tried to. "You sound like you're feeling better."

"I am, although I don't think I can get up yet. I'll probably have to sleep down here tonight."

Aw, crap. She was staying the night. Which brought up the issue of *where* she was going to sleep.

Good thing he'd brought the mattress in here for her—it was too cold in the bedroom. Where he would sleep, Max didn't know, but he'd figure something out.

"Give me a second," he told her.

He came back in, clutching a pillow.

"Wait." Sasha scrambled to sit up. "Is that *your* pillow?" She looked around as if expecting more to appear. Her voice dropped to a whisper. "Is there only one bedroom?"

"There's only one me, so yes."

She stared down at the mattress. "Only one bed," she said to herself. She rubbed her arms like she was trying to wake herself up. Like this was a nightmare.

Max felt his temper rising. Yeah, she'd been through a lot and this place wasn't exactly cozy, but it was what he had. It wasn't like he was running a bed-and-breakfast here. The animals had the shelter they needed, and that was all Max cared about. He hadn't invited her here, for heaven's sake.

Okay, so maybe his reaction was a bit much, but he'd had a hell of a day. So had she though.

He crossed his arms. "Yeah. One bed. And it's yours."

She blinked up at him. "But where will you sleep? I can't take your bed."

Oh. So that's what she was upset about. He let his arms

fall. "It's fine. I'll find a sleeping bag. You need it more than me, and the bedroom would be too cold for you."

"If the bedroom is so cold, how do you stand it? Do you have a space heater?"

Her concern made his skin prickle. No one besides his mom had cared this much about whether he was warm in ages. Or maybe it had only been his mom ever. He didn't date much—no time what with the horses and the rest of his animals and building the house—but the people he did date weren't at all concerned if he was warm at night.

"No space heater." He spooned soup into a bowl for her. "There's only electricity in the barn, not here." He cut a slice of bread for her too. "I run hot—I don't need a heater."

"Even in a thousand-year blizzard?"

His hand tightened on the plate he was about to give her. She wasn't actually asking him to share the mattress on the floor with her, but that was all he could think about.

She's sick, asshole. And she almost died. She didn't choose this.

Max believed in a code, the way a man ought to behave with those he was responsible for. His father had instilled it in him, showing Max how a woman ought to be treated. Max's father worshipped his mother. And honestly, his mom deserved it. His dad expected Max to treat all women with equal respect. His mom did too.

Max would never let his parents down by ignoring his code or avoiding his responsibilities. And he was definitely responsible for Sasha now. He'd given his little cousin a long talk about it when Fidel had come to him with a sticky situation involving a drunk girl—she'd come on to Fidel, but he hadn't quite felt right about it even though he thought she was smoking hot. So he'd turned her down.

Max had told him he'd done the right thing. And that a

real man didn't say yes to every opportunity to hook up with a girl—he said no when it was hard but right.

Somehow Max had become the relationship guy for all the younger men in his family. Probably because he wasn't married or paired up. He must *know* things, right?

Right now it was damned difficult to remember his own advice. If she offered to share the bed, freely, of her own choice... he'd say no. Because it would be the right thing to do. No matter how tempted he was.

He released a long exhale. "I'll be fine. Soup's ready."

Sasha slowly sat up as he handed her the plate. And immediately dropped it.

"Sorry," she muttered. "Sitting up makes me dizzy."

Thank goodness he'd only handed her the bread. Poinsettia sniffed at the slice before Max pulled it away.

"That's not for you," he told the calf. Then to Sasha, "Don't worry about it. Got plenty of bread. Do you want to try to sit in the chair?"

She eyed the one chair in the room. "I don't know."

He racked his brains, thinking of something to prop her up against. She already had the only pillow. There were some horse blankets out in the barn, but they weren't exactly clean. The tack room did have an ancient couch in it, but hauling it into the house wasn't going to work, not with all that snow between here and there.

The solution that did occur to him made his entire body tighten. *Cool it.* "Um." He cleared his throat. "We don't have a lot of options here. But—and you can say no"—*please say no*—"you could sit propped up on me. And I could help you eat."

He tried to sound as nonchalant as he could, as if he offered this kind of nursing every day. Mostly he sounded

29

incredibly uncomfortable, which he was. He had a profound new appreciation for Fidel's dilemma right now.

Sasha looked down at her hands, her cheeks going pink. "That's... that's really nice of you. I should probably try to sit up again. Really, I'm just being lazy." But she stayed propped on one elbow, her color wan under her blush.

"You're not lazy," he ground out. "You almost died. Let me think of something else—"

"Okay, we can try it." She said it in a rush as if she expected him to change his mind. Or maybe she thought *she* might. "I just feel bad that I'm being such a pain."

"You're not." He crouched down, trying to figure out how best to do this. "It's not like I had big plans for today."

"You certainly didn't plan for *this*."

He hadn't, but they'd make the best of it. "I'll sit on the edge of the mattress, and you can scoot between my legs. If that's okay."

They'd be uncomfortably close, but he couldn't think of a better way to do it. If he held her up with one arm, that only left him the other hand to help her eat with. He was probably going to have to hold the bowl for her too.

"Sure." Her tone was oddly strained. Probably because he, a total stranger, was about to manhandle her. Again.

And he'd removed her clothes. Which was not something he should be lingering over when he was about to hold her close.

They managed to maneuver into position without once making eye contact, which Max counted as a blessing. He was already too aware of the scent of her skin, the rise and fall of her breaths, the way her hair feathered over her shoulders. If he met her gaze this close to her, it'd be impossible to maintain his composure like he needed to.

Finally she was between his legs. *Keep it cool, buddy.*

Slowly she leaned back, her hair brushing his chin. Her back met his chest, his arms coming around her.

It was then he realized this was an absolutely awful idea.

Sasha's head was spinning, and it wasn't because she was finally sitting up.

Max was so solid and warm behind her, and she could feel the strength in his arms as they came around her to steady her, and it was... She swallowed hard, her pulse fluttering in her throat.

He was only trying to help her because she was too weak to sit up on her own. That was all. He was being nice, and she was being a bother. Once she was out of here, this moment would be something she'd laugh about with Pippa. *And then he practically hugged me as he fed me! Isn't that wild?*

At least she'd be laughing outwardly—inside, she'd be remembering it wistfully.

This was like something out of one of her fantasies, being tenderly cradled like this and cared for while she was sick. She almost wanted to cry.

The last time Sasha had gotten sick, the closest she'd come to a comforting hug had been a FaceTime call with her mom. Pippa had brought her chicken soup in between running from her first job to her second, but Sasha had had to heat it up all on her own. As she'd eaten her soup on the couch, shivering from her fever, she'd imagined what it would be like to have someone like Max take care of her. To put his hand to her brow and worry over her. To put the thermometer in her mouth and cluck when he saw the reading. To pull her close and share his body heat.

She was grateful for her mom and Pippa's efforts, but Max holding her like this was something else entirely. Beyond even her small fantasies.

Poinsettia watched them with wide eyes, like she was asking, *What are you two doing?*

Okay, a calf watching wasn't part of the fantasy. But she was so cute Sasha couldn't imagine her not being here.

And okay, Max was only doing it to be nice and because she'd practically collapsed on his doorstep. He wasn't doing it because he was madly in love with her and she was the air in his lungs and seeing her hurt tore him into a hundred million bloody pieces. Not at all.

He didn't want to do this. He was being forced into it, and he wasn't fantasizing about how wonderful and comforting this moment was.

Because of that, Sasha didn't let herself enjoy the fantasy. She had to be serious here, just like her mom always warned. No daydreaming. She focused on sitting up on her own, which was harder than she expected, and eating her soup, which was downright impossible.

"Sorry," she muttered as she dropped the spoon for the second time.

"Can I help?" His breath brushed across her cheek. He reached for the spoon, his hand hovering over it.

"Yes. Please."

He picked up the spoon, dipped it in the bowl. The soup smelled so rich, so comforting, but with a tingle of something more. Not spicy, but spice.

And his hand... She couldn't look away. Heavy, blunt fingers, a strong wrist, dark hair scattered across his forearm, but he moved with fluidity. She supposed he had to be strong as well as deft to train horses.

How did someone get into that?

He brought the spoon slowly to her mouth, giving her plenty of time to aim for it. She wobbled even though he was holding her up and put her hand to his wrist to steady herself.

If she were feeling normal, her pulse would have kicked into overdrive. His skin was warm, smooth, the bones beneath strong, steady. As it was, her heart gave a weak flutter.

"Got it?" he murmured.

She gave a short nod and closed her lips over the spoon. Oh. *Oh.*

She was suddenly aware of just how long it had been since she'd eaten and how badly she needed this. The soup was rich but not heavy, that spice she'd smelled tickling the back of her tongue. She closed her eyes because it was just that good.

"Okay?" he asked. "Want more?"

"Yes please. It's delicious, and I'm starving."

He helped her eat some more, then handed her a slice of bread. "Can you handle this on your own?"

"Yeah." Her hand was weak and shaky, but she managed it. The bread was warm, soft on the inside, with just the right amount of butter. "Did you make this butter too?"

He laughed softly. She felt it all through her back, his amusement. "No. But maybe someday."

"I remember in this book I read as a kid"—she took another spoonful of soup from him—"the little girl in the story had to churn butter. And she hated it. It made her arms tired."

Sasha was feeling tired again too, her eyes drooping. The soup was so good though, and she wanted to finish it and the bread. And to enjoy being close to someone like this. Being taken care of.

Her mom was probably the last person who'd fed her when she was sick. If only Sasha had somehow figured out how to go home for Christmas, she'd be with her mom and not half-frozen and sleeping on Max's floor. He was being so patient, feeding her as if he did it all the time. As if this wasn't weird and he wasn't aware of how close and intimate they were.

She was being a pain in the neck, and he was being an absolute prince. Okay, he was kind of curt with her at first, but he'd had an awful day. Anyone would be crabby. Really, she was glad he was the one who'd saved her.

Now that she had some food in her, her awareness was like a butterfly testing out new wings, fluttering unsteadily this way and that. The tensing of his pecs against her shoulder as he moved. The hint of peppermint on his breath as he exhaled into her hair. How safe she felt, sleepy and stomach full and warm under her favorite blanket.

It was what she imagined falling in love might feel like.

Don't start making up stories.

That was what she did though, spun out fantasies about anything and everything. Especially when she was falling asleep. That was the best time to let her mind run free. To spin out things that could never happen but would be wonderful if they did.

She was so sleepy though. The soup was warm in her belly, her mouth tasted of butter, and Max was a solid, comforting presence against her.

"I'm done," she managed to mumble.

He leaned closer, moved the bowl away.

He kissed the side of her neck, light but lingering. His arms tightened around her as if he'd never let go. "You gave me a scare today. I can't imagine living without you. But you're here now and safe. So get some rest. Sleep."

So she did.

3

She'd fallen asleep in his arms.

Max held her carefully, not wanting to wake her. She must still be in bad shape if she could fall asleep like this. But at least she'd eaten something.

Food and sleep were probably the best things for her now. At least they were all he could give her what with the snow and lack of cell service.

This close to her, he could see that her hair wasn't merely brown—the strands varied from gold to nearly black. Her nose wasn't delicate, but he liked it. It gave her character. And her mouth was wide, but that just made her smile all the better.

He sighed. He ought to put her down. It was inappropriate to hold her like this and think about how pretty she was. To imagine settling her across his lap. Laying the both of them down and cradling her as she dreamed.

That went against everything in his code, to take advantage like that. She needed help, not whatever he was imagining.

"I'm going to put her down," he told Poinsettia. Mostly to nudge himself into doing it.

The calf licked her nose. He couldn't tell if she believed him or not.

"I have to check on your mom too. See if she's feeling better."

Poinsettia laid her head back down. Really, she was the prettiest calf. Prettier than her mama, not that he'd ever tell Petunia that.

"All right. Time to get to it." But he held Sasha a moment longer, enjoying the simple comfort of it. It had taken something terrible to get her here, but he had to admit, his Christmas was looking a little brighter because of her.

When the thaw came, she'd leave. She had to; she had no place here. But Max realized he'd miss her when she did. She was funny, charming, and she'd clearly fallen in love with the calf. How was he supposed to resist that?

Well, he'd keep his infatuation to himself. She needed to focus on recovering.

He eased her down to the mattress, taking the time to tuck the blanket around her. The stove was warm, and her color was better, but he couldn't risk her catching a chill.

While she slept, he made another bottle for Poinsettia, who drank it down eagerly, then fell asleep herself. Sasha and the calf made quite the picture together, sleeping in front of the stove.

Once that was done, he ate a quick bite himself, standing up at the stove, then went out to feed lunch to everyone else.

The horses were restless, unhappy at being stuck inside for so long. They settled a bit when they got some hay, but Max knew they'd be complaining again before long. He couldn't blame them. He was agitated himself, ready to get all this snow gone and get back to their usual routine.

Sasha would be leaving then though. Yes, he wanted to get back to his life, but he also wanted to enjoy her company a little longer. He'd liked talking to her when he'd helped her eat. Yes, she was pretty, and yes, she felt right in his arms—but she was funny too. And warm and kind. And she wasn't too upset that he'd put her on the floor next to a baby calf.

Once the horses and the other cows were fed, Max went to check on Petunia. When he saw she was still down, he blew out a heavy sigh of frustration. He couldn't let her go on too much longer like this. She was suffering and it wasn't fair. But damn did he want to give her another chance to come back. If only he'd been able to make it, to find the vet and get more calcium...

But he hadn't. He'd saved Sasha instead. So maybe this was the way it was meant to be—Sasha survived, but Petunia didn't.

Max wasn't quite ready to accept that bargain though, not yet. Saving both of them was what he wanted. He walked into the stall, the straw bedding crackling under his boots. It was warm and sweet-smelling with the new straw he'd put down, wanting it to be as nice as possible for Petunia. Might not help her recover, but it wouldn't hurt.

He rubbed at the white diamond on her forehead. "Come on," he said, urging her to get better. "You've got to get up, fight this thing. Poinsettia needs you."

Petunia blinked in question at him.

"That's what Sasha named your baby. Poinsettia. A perfect Christmas name for a perfect Christmas calf."

Petunia seemed to accept that. She blinked again.

"Sasha is the woman I found at the end of the drive.

Half-frozen, nearly dead. Scared the crap out of me when I tripped over her when I was pulling out. And it was damned lucky I was there." He scratched at her white mark, knowing she liked that. "Thanks to you, I guess. Otherwise I never would have gone out."

Petunia stared back with that utter calmness she had. Some of Max's lingering fear over Sasha drained away. He could remember that moment in the driveway, frantically digging her out of the snow, praying she was somehow still alive, without wanting to puke now.

Holding her close as she ate had helped, he realized. He knew on a physical level just how alive and vital she was.

Sasha was going to be okay; he was pretty sure. Petunia was less certain.

"Want to try to get up?" He reached for the cow's lead rope. "Come on. Let's just try."

He pulled, urging her to get up, to prove she was going to make it. Petunia got one leg under her, then another, hoisting her back end up and going onto her front knees.

"Come on." Max's heart was in his throat. She was so close. If he could just get her on her feet, it would be a win. "Come on, girl. You can do it."

Petunia remained there for a moment, suspended between up and down. Max never let off the pressure on her halter, urging her upward with everything in him. Physically he wouldn't make a difference, not against a cow almost ten times his weight, but mentally it might. If hopes could lift her up, he was hoping his hardest.

Slowly she began to sink back down. Like a ship sinking beneath the waves—gradual, then all at once. And about as unstoppable too.

"Damn." Max released the lead rope, his heart plummeting as hard as Petunia had. "Damn."

His throat closed, but that was the most emotion he'd allow himself. He wasn't giving up on her yet.

"Good job," he told her, rubbing her head. "You did so good. Next time we'll get you up. I promise. You keep fighting, and I'll keep trying. And once you're up, which you will be soon, Poinsettia will come back out here with you. She'll be so happy to see her mama again."

Petunia sighed, looking as if the effort had taken a lot out of her. That was a bad sign.

"All right," Max said. "We'll try again later."

He checked her water and her feed, made sure she was up on her belly enough and not on her side. Everything was as good as he could make it.

And it still wasn't enough.

"I'll be back," he promised the cow.

As he walked out, he prayed for a Christmas miracle here. He'd gotten one when he rescued Sasha—surely there was enough Christmas magic out there for one more for Petunia.

Otherwise when the thaw came, he'd be saying goodbye not only to Sasha but to Petunia as well.

When Sasha woke up, it was dark.

For a moment her mind darted frantically, trying to make sense of her surroundings. She had just fallen asleep so it should still be light out... but it wasn't.

She knew where she was at least. On the floor in front of the stove on Max's only bed. *Only one bed.*

She shuddered and shook her head. Now wasn't the time for that. How long had she been asleep? She felt tired, but it was the kind of tired that came from lying around too much. A lazy kind of tired.

She sat up, rubbed her eyes. Her head ached dully behind her eyes, enough to let her know things weren't one hundred percent in her body. But not so bad that she wanted to fall back asleep.

"Poinsettia?" she called. "Max?"

There was a scrabbling sound next to her. A warm, furry head butted under her hand.

"Oh good." She gave the calf a scratch. "You're still here. Or maybe not. Maybe it's better that you go back with your mom, except she's still sick."

"Mom's still sick."

Sasha spun around to find Max sitting at a small table in the corner, an honest-to-goodness oil lamp providing light and a notebook and pen in front of him.

Western romance, her mind provided. *We only have an oil lamp to light our evenings. And no TV. So we'll have to entertain ourselves the old-fashioned way.*

In the only bed in the house.

Okay, she really needed to stop now. Sasha rubbed her eyes to get rid of the lingering images in her mind.

"I'm sorry about Petunia," she said. "Is the snow cleared up? Can you get out yet?"

He shook his head. "Still packed in. How are you feeling?" He rose from the table, the lamplight casting golden highlights and soft shadows over his length.

"Better." She ran a hand across her forehead. "You know how sometimes you're sick, and you have that one last sleep, the one that makes everything better? And you wake up and still don't feel great, but you just know you're getting well? Yeah. I think I had that kind of nap."

"Good." He came to crouch next to her. "Your color is better. No fever?"

She shook her head, feeling suddenly shy with him so close. Which was strange because he'd held her in his arms to feed her, for heaven's sake. "Thank you. For taking care of me. I know I must have ruined your Christmas plans. I certainly ruined mine."

He didn't smile at her weak joke. "What were your plans?"

"Usually I go back to visit my family in Florida. I grew up outside Miami, right where it almost stops being the Atlantic and becomes the Gulf," she explained. "But flights were too expensive this year. Well, they're too expensive every year, but my car needed repairs, so I didn't have the money." She picked at the blanket. "I guess I'm going to have even more repairs after this."

Again, she tried to make it a joke. Again, he didn't smile.

"I'll tow it out for you with the tractor," he said. "And it might be just fine. You never know."

Max was trying to make her feel better. It was so sweet she almost smiled. Look at the two of them—her trying to lighten the mood with silly jokes and him refusing to smile, instead promising to tow her car.

"Can the tractor drive in the snow?" she asked. "Like a snowplow?"

"Probably not," he said. "I only use it to drag the arena." He frowned for a moment. "I don't even think there's a snowplow within two hours of here. Maybe some in Pine Ridge, but even they never get snow like *this*."

Right, there weren't any snowplows here. Not that there were any at home either. "We have hurricanes at home," she said, "but never any snow. I guess that's why I was dumb enough to go walking out into a blizzard."

42

Max's expression was serious. "You could have just as easily frozen to death in the car too."

The concern in his tone warmed her all the way to her toes, hotter even than the fire in the stove.

"Why did you drive up if you knew it was going to storm?" he asked.

She flushed. "I probably shouldn't have I thought it would just be really cold. And... well, it's been too expensive for me to go home for a couple of years now. I didn't want to spend Christmas alone again. A dumb reason to risk my life, I guess."

"It's not dumb." His tone was quiet but deep. "Even I get lonely sometimes."

She could imagine, what with him being so isolated out here. She actually didn't even know how far they were from the highway. If he had no cell signal, it could be pretty far. Even with his horses and cows, he must want someone to talk to sometimes. Someone to touch and to touch him.

"Why don't you have a dog?" she blurted out, trying to run her thoughts off that particular track, which wouldn't end up anywhere good. "It seems like you should have one."

"I lost Gwen last year," he said. "I haven't had the heart to get a new one."

She swallowed hard. "Oh. I'm so sorry. I have a dog at home, but with renting, it's just too hard to have any kind of pet here."

"What's its name? What kind of dog?"

"Andy. He's some kind of beagle mix." Sasha smiled as she thought of him. "He's got a very distinctive call, this sort of cross between a howl and a bark. Like he can't decide what noise to make, so he'll make them both." Her smile faded. "I really miss him. And my mom and dad and my sister and brother."

"Of course you do." His expression was warm with sympathy. Warmer than she'd ever thought he could be based on their first meeting. "How did you end up out here?"

"I wanted something different. But I can't handle the cold"—she gave a short, ironic laugh—"and I still wanted to be close to the ocean. So when I wanted to move far away and be on my own, that didn't leave a ton of options. I didn't expect to get stuck out here so long." She rubbed her eyes, trying to stop the tears before they started. "It's just hard. To not be able to go home for so long." She pulled in a shaky breath. "What about you? Is your family close by?"

"About two hours north, in Norco. Hang on." He went into his bedroom and came back with a fistful of tissues. She accepted them gratefully. "I was going to spend Christmas morning with them, but Petunia and the weather had other plans. I've got four siblings, about a dozen aunts and uncles, and dozens of cousins, not to mention my nieces and nephews, so it's a big celebration each year. Lots of food and noise and gifts."

"It sounds wonderful," she said wistfully as she dabbed at her nose. "I'm sorry you can't get home this year."

"I'm sorry you can't." He was watching her from the little table, the lamp flickering next to him. Something about his expression, the intensity of it, made her breath catch.

"It's Christmas Eve tomorrow, isn't it?"

He nodded.

If everything had gone according to plan, Sasha would have been at Pippa's place by now. She'd have exclaimed over the goats and chickens, and there would have been a tiny tree with tiny lights on the table in the RV Pippa was living in. There would have been mulled wine since that was something they'd gotten into two Christmases ago. And presents and laughter.

And Sasha would have asked how Ansel—the cousin Pippa had tried to set Sasha up with—was doing with his new girlfriend. Pippa would have been cuddling with Bear, her own personal romance hero. And Lulu, Pippa's sister, would have been there with her own boyfriend.

It would have been fun and festive, but in many ways, Sasha still would have been alone.

Max would have been able to get the calcium, and Petunia would have been fine. Poinsettia could have been with her mom for Christmas. And Max would have spent Christmas Day with his mom and dad and siblings and all the rest of them.

Sasha had never had a holiday quite like that, where you could get lost in a crowd of family, but it sounded nice. Overwhelming but loving.

She wiped her eyes. Okay, she was missing her family and he was missing his. But they still had each other. This might not be the holiday either of them wanted, but maybe something special could still happen.

"We should do something," she said. "Find some pine boughs and decorate. Maybe even a tree. Cook up a feast just for us." She realized she was babbling, but as she went on and he didn't say anything, she realized he might hate the idea. She was just some woman he'd rescued, and here she was planning a Christmas for him. Maybe he just wanted to miss his big, warm family Christmas and not play pretend with her. "Or not. You probably have chores and stuff. I can just hang out here too."

An odd, small smile played around the corners of his mouth like he was touched by her nervousness but didn't want her to know. Or maybe he didn't want her to know he wanted to laugh at her.

"It's a good idea," he said gravely. "There's a stand of pine trees about a twenty-minute walk from here. I don't have any decorations, but I could find some candles at least."

Relief rushed through her. He liked the idea. He wanted to help. "I can make some. If you have string or paper and scissors and some glue—pretty much anything—I can whip some things up." Even something simple like a paper chain would go a long way to making it feel more like Christmas.

"I'm sure I can find something," he said. "And we can go through the freezer and the pantry and see what we can pull together for a feast. We might as well make the best of it if we're going to be snowed in together."

But it didn't sound like he was just making the best of it —it sounded like he was enjoying himself.

Snowed in together. He couldn't know what that meant to a romance reader, but it sent hot shudders down Sasha's spine. Snowed in together for Christmas. Only one bed. Rescued by a hot cowboy. Who had a literal calf in his kitchen.

Okay, maybe that had never been in a romance novel she'd ever read, but it should have been. It turned out baby cows were much, much cuter than dogs.

"Yeah," she said breathlessly, "we should."

For a moment they seemed to hold their breath together. He had such lovely dark eyes, deep as... Well, she couldn't think of a good phrase right now. But very, very deep. That was the trouble with eyes like his—you had to see them to know how it felt to look *into* them, to understand. Words couldn't really do them justice. Not even all the words she'd read in her books.

"I should be turning in," he said, deep and slow.

She blinked, trying to come out of the spell. But he'd said he had to *turn in,* and that was something only cowboys in books said, or at least she'd thought so. It was hard to remember she wasn't in some fantasy when he acted like that.

Her eyes widened as the meaning hit her. Oh, he was going to go sleep on the floor in his freezing bedroom. He was going to give her the only mattress and the warmest spot in the house and go sleep alone on the coldest night in a hundred years. Maybe even a thousand years.

It was silly. He said she might freeze to death in her car; well, he might freeze to death in that bedroom. They were both adults, both capable of behaving themselves. There was no reason they couldn't share a bed. It wasn't like they'd somehow kiss each other accidentally. Or more. They would each take a side of the bed and never cross to the other side. They'd be little islands under the blanket.

She gathered up her courage, looked straight into his eyes, heart pounding like rocks in a tumble dryer, and said, "We can share the bed. I insist. It will be perfectly fine."

4

I t will be perfectly fine.

Max was pretty sure it damn well wouldn't. With the lamplight slipping over her skin, caressing her curves, he felt far from fine. He was twisted up, turned out, itching to touch or—better yet—taste her.

Judging by her calm, steady expression, she didn't feel the same. She was only thinking about decorating for Christmas and staying warm as she slept. And not being a bother to him.

Too late. He was so hot and bothered by her suggestion he ought to stalk out right now and spend the night in the barn.

"I told you," he growled, "I run hot. I'll be just fine in the bedroom."

She blinked like he'd snapped at her. "Don't be ridiculous. The bedroom will be too cold, and you don't have to give me the only bed out of some sense of... of... chivalry."

She said the word like it was so old-fashioned it was laughable. But she was wrong—Max might not be the most polished guy, but he had a code he lived by. Same as his dad had and same as his grandpa had. Sasha was his to protect as long as she was here. And the best way to protect her was to keep out of her bed. Even if it was usually *his* bed.

He shook his head. "No. It's not happening. Go to sleep."

Her chin jutted out. "It's going to be well below freezing tonight. You said I could die in the car—is your bedroom that much warmer? And what if Poinsettia needs something in the middle of the night?"

The calf looked up at her name. When her eyes met Max's, they seemed to say, *Yeah, what about that?*

"I'll have to get up every few hours to feed her anyway," he said. "And to check on Petunia. So I'd be waking you up if we did share a bed."

"I sleep like the dead."

It was true—she'd barely moved during the several-hour nap she'd just taken. He'd had to stare long and hard at her a few times to make sure she was still breathing. His heart had stopped until he was sure she was okay each and every time.

"It's not right," he muttered. Okay, maybe he was too old-fashioned. But— "It's just not appropriate. Me sleeping with you."

Oh, but he wanted to. He'd only met her this morning, only found out how pretty she was a few hours ago, and already he had it bad for her. It was the way she treated the calf and how she wanted to make a Christmas celebration and how honest she was about missing her family.

She was sweet and open, and yeah, saving her life had done something to him. Made him feel oddly possessive of her.

"I trust you," she said finally. "You dug me half-frozen out of the snow and saved my life. You only want to help me, not hurt me. And I want to repay you in some small way. With the Christmas decorations and with this." She patted the space next to her. "I won't be able to sleep, knowing that you're suffering in the other room. And I know you won't do anything I don't want."

She couldn't know how that sounded. She just couldn't. He swallowed hard, trying not to think about all the things he wanted to do with her. Things she might want if he asked nicely.

Or not. She had barely escaped death not more than twelve hours ago. Sleep was the only thing on her mind.

He'd make sure it was the only thing on his. Assuming he managed to sleep at all.

"Fine," he barked, not caring if he sounded pissed. Anger would create a much-needed barrier between them. "I've got to go do the night check. You should get some rest."

He walked out without waiting for her reply. He made sure to linger over his chores even though it was colder than the Arctic in the barn. He double-checked blankets, made sure the horses had food through the night—food in their bellies would help keep them warm—took his time looking over the herd of cattle penned in the arena. The animals would be cold tonight no doubt, but they wouldn't be in any danger. Finally he went to the milk cows.

Mopsy was lying down with her calf, half dozing as she chewed her cud. Max wondered if it was time to give up and just get Mopsy to foster Poinsettia. He'd hoped Petunia would recover and take care of her own calf—he liked for his cows to raise their own babies, it seemed to make them happy—but maybe it was time to let go of that hope and do what was best for Poinsettia.

It would be work to get Mopsy to accept the calf though —he couldn't just dump Poinsettia in with Mopsy and let nature take its course. Mopsy knew Poinsettia wasn't her baby, and she wouldn't be happy to have Petunia's offspring nursing off her. Max would have to watch them closely at first.

But he'd already promised Sasha they'd prepare for Christmas tomorrow. So maybe he'd hold off putting Poinsettia with Mopsy a bit longer.

When he came to Petunia's stall, he gasped. *She was up.*

"Hey, baby," he said as he walked in. "You look better."

Standing up was good. It was great.

She watched him with a lowered head, her breathing labored. She might be up, but she wasn't one hundred percent. He looked into her grain bucket—she'd eaten some. And her water bucket was half-empty.

He tossed her more hay and refilled her water, watching her the entire time. Petunia stayed on her feet, but she looked tired. Not quite herself.

"I'm going to grab Poinsettia," he told her. "Stay here."

Sasha was already asleep when he came in, her head pillowed on her folded hands. She'd left the only pillow for him.

He'd have to fix that later. For now he needed to get the calf.

Poinsettia came easily, licking at his face. She was somehow small and heavy at the same time. Even with the path he'd cut to the barn, it was slow, hard going through the snow.

When he put the calf under Petunia's nose, she gave a glad lowing noise, same as any mother would when she saw her baby again. Poinsettia let her mother lick her all over. It reminded Max of how his mom hugged him, long and glad.

Poinsettia eventually made her way back to the udder. As she latched on, her tail started wagging, the sign of a happy baby. Max made sure everything was going well, then decided to leave them alone. They knew what to do.

"I'll be back in an hour or so to check on you," he told Petunia.

The walk back to the house was much easier than the walk out. No calf in his arms and no worry for Petunia weighing on him. Things were finally looking better.

Sasha was still asleep when he walked in. He watched her for a few moments, the way her breath moved the strands of hair across her face, how her fingers curled and uncurled with whatever she was dreaming about.

He wanted to wake her up and tell her what had happened. Or better yet, take her out to the barn to see for herself.

But she was still sick, and she needed her rest, not a trip outside in below-zero conditions. It could wait until morning.

In his bedroom, which was empty without his mattress, he changed into a T-shirt and some sweatpants. For a moment he considered sleeping in there anyway. There was a sleeping bag somewhere in his horse trailer—he could find it and roll himself up in it. Sasha would probably never know.

But the floor was frigid against his feet even through his socks, and he was already shivering. She was right—he'd freeze in this room.

I trust you. She'd given him that speech about saving her and her wanting to give back. It would be crappy of him to sleep in here after she did that.

Like she'd said, they were both adults. Nothing would happen.

Still, he climbed carefully, quietly under the covers, doing his best not to touch or disturb her. Trying to pretend she wasn't there even though every inch of his skin crackled with awareness of her. The sheets were too rough on his skin, the blanket too heavy. It was like his entire body had been zapped awake.

This was the warmest spot in the house. The fire in the stove was low but still going, and it spread heat over them like another blanket. He considered the pillow and what to do with it. He meant to give it back to her, but that would wake her up. Still, he couldn't take it for himself.

In the end, he put it between them. There—a nice, safe wall to separate him from her.

Max checked that the alarm on his phone was set to go off in an hour—he had to check on Petunia and Poinsettia again—then tucked himself under the blankets. Next to him, Sasha breathed with regular, delicate inhales and exhales.

The blanket she'd brought with her looked like something his grandmother might have knitted. It smelled like Christmas at her house somehow, like sugar and cinnamon and a hint of pine. And it was warm as heck. Way warmer than it should have been, which might have been why it saved Sasha's life...

The alarm snapped him awake. He tried to reach out to shut it off, but his arm was stuck. He rolled over, used his other arm, blindly reaching out.

The noise died.

He rolled back, reluctantly coming up out of sleep. It was so warm. And it smelled good. Like flowers.

That was when he realized he was holding Sasha.

Her back was pressed against his chest, her butt cradled in his pelvis, their legs fitted together as neat as two spoons. The arm that he couldn't move was under her neck. The arm that he could move had somehow found its way over her waist.

She was sleeping as soundly as ever. Not even his flailing had woken her up. She wasn't lying about sleeping like the dead.

But then how had they ended up like this? It wasn't just him pulling her into his body, was it? And where was the protective pillow he'd put down?

She murmured in her sleep and wriggled into him, her soft parts making him hard as a nail.

"Sasha." He couldn't seem to move. But he could try to wake her up. "Sasha."

"Hmm?" She rolled over, blinked her eyes half-open. A smile curved her mouth. "Oh, it's *you*."

Christ, had a woman greeted him in that tone ever? Like she was so pleased and surprised and turned on all at once.

"Sasha. You need to—"

He'd meant to tell her she needed to move over, away from him, but she took the opportunity to bury her face in his chest instead. When she inhaled deeply, like she was drinking him in, he was lost. Totally lost in her and the way she was.

He cupped her jaw, lifted her face to his. "Sweetheart." His voice was gravelly. "You have to wake up."

She looked straight up at him. "I am. I was dreaming and then the alarm went off..." Her gaze flicked down. "Oh dear. I didn't mean—"

"I think I did it," he said quickly, not wanting her to take the blame. His hand refused to release his hold on her though. "I'm sorry."

"Don't be," she said. "Not on my account."

She wasn't moving away. His arm was around her, his

hand holding her face, her legs tangled with his... and this was clearly where she wanted to be.

He wanted her to be here too.

"I know I said nothing would happen," he said.

"I said it too."

"But something did happen."

Her calf, trapped between his legs, flexed. Her hand slid up his chest and around to cup the back of his neck. He was still and hard as stone.

"I read a lot of romance," she said as if that explained something. "Can I kiss you?"

He'd never had a woman ask before, and it was hot as hell. Because obviously he wanted to kiss her, but to have her just come out and ask was something else.

"Of course," he said. "But first, can I kiss *you?*"

Her laugh sparkled through the air. "Wait," she said. "We'll go at the same time. One."

"Two."

"Three."

Their eyes were open when their mouths met. Sasha's kiss was as soft and sweet as she was. He couldn't see the details of her eyes—the light from the stove was too low—but they were dark pools, her lashes thick and sooty.

Her eyes fluttered closed, her lashes brushing her cheeks. Her mouth parted in clear invitation. She gave a small exhale that might have been a *please*.

She didn't have to beg him. He closed his eyes and deepened the kiss, his tongue meeting hers.

An electric rush moved through him. He groaned, his fingers on her jaw tightening. He had to be careful, remember to hold back with her, but it was so hard. Her legs moved restlessly between his, her hand on his neck in an iron grip.

She didn't want him to hold back. Her eagerness fed the fire in him.

He shifted so that she was over him, the better to give his hungry hands access to her. The underside of her breast fit the curve between his thumb and forefinger perfectly. The notch of her waist enticed him to stroke again and again. The jut of her hip was made for his grip.

When she bent to join their mouths, her hair made a curtain around them, the silken ends caressing his face. Her mouth was hot and needy on his, her hands fisted into his shirt. She wasn't holding back a thing, and her response surged through him. It was like they were directly connected everywhere they touched, no separation between what he was feeling and what she was.

He'd never had a kiss this hot, this consuming. And it was only their first one. He'd never get enough of her kisses.

But she'd be leaving soon no matter what.

It was that fact that made him gently ease his mouth from hers. She made a not-so-tiny noise of protest, blindly seeking his mouth again, which almost broke him. But he managed to hold firm.

Slowly Sasha blinked open her eyes. Even in the low light, he could see her lips were swollen, ripe-looking. "Wow."

"Yeah." He rubbed his thumb over her full bottom lip. "But you're still recovering."

She nipped at his thumb. "I'm feeling better."

Probably she was, but not well enough for what he wanted to do with her. "Keep getting better, and I promise more kissing. Among other things."

He ran the back of his fingers along her cheek, so soft, so velvety. He wanted to stroke every inch of her, taste those same spots, but... she was still too weak. Still recuperating.

"You need to rest." He kept his tone as gentle and light as his touch on her cheek. "And I need to check the barn."

She blinked long and slow. "I like kissing you." She already sounded half-asleep. "I don't want to stop."

What that did to his heart and other parts of him... He swallowed hard, told his body to calm down. "I don't want to either. But you need to get better. You're already falling asleep."

In fact, her eyes were closing. She smiled anyway. "I guess." That came out both amused and piqued. It almost made him kiss her again.

Instead, he helped her back onto the pillow, tucking the blankets firmly around her. And he made himself march out into the cold, dark night and away from her sweet warmth.

5

Sasha wriggled her toes under the blanket. They were cold even with her socks. But they shouldn't be. They'd been so warm when Poinsettia had been on them.

She came awake in a rush. "Poinsettia!" She snapped up, clutching the blanket.

No Poinsettia. No Max.

"Oh no." Her pulse hammered through her as a sickening rush of anxiety made her moan. "Where is she?"

If the little calf was gone, did that mean...?

"Sasha?" Max's voice came from the bedroom. "You okay?" He dashed over to her, putting a hand to her forehead. "What happened? You look..."

Sasha grabbed his wrist. "Where's Poinsettia?" Tears sprang to her eyes. "Is she okay? She seemed fine last night."

Max sighed with relief. "She's good. Petunia's back up, so she's back with her mom. You were asleep when I took her out to the barn."

"Oh." Sasha let her hand drop. That was great news, but she still felt a pinch near her heart. She'd miss her little companion. But being reunited with her mom was the best thing for her. "Petunia is okay then?"

She might be way too invested in a cow she'd never even seen. Still, she waited on a knife's edge for his answer.

"Seems to be on her way to recovery. She was so happy to see Poinsettia again." He remained crouched beside her, his jeans straining over his thighs. He stroked her hair back from her face. "How are you doing?"

His tone had gone all deep and soft, and she knew he was remembering their kiss. She'd had dreams all night about it and about him holding her close, keeping her warm and safe.

Keep getting better, he'd said. Well, she felt pretty darn good right now. Ready for more kisses for sure.

"Great. How are you?"

He smiled like he knew what she was thinking. "Had the best sleep of my life last night. So pretty good."

"Really?" She licked her lips, and his gaze followed the movement. It made heat flush through her. "That seems like something people just say. Like in books, at least the books I read, you find the one and then everything is perfect."

She flushed even harder as she realized what she'd said. He was going to think she was trying to tell him he loved her. Or she loved him.

Of course, he was pretty amazing. Maybe at first she hadn't quite been able to see him as a romance hero, but after last night, she could definitely see him as *her* romance hero.

He didn't look freaked out by what she'd just said though. "I'm telling the truth—it really was the best sleep of my life. I don't know about the book stuff. I only know how I feel. And what I said was true."

That had to mean something. Because even though

she'd had one of the worst experiences of her life yesterday when she'd crashed the car, she felt rested. Safe. Right where she should be.

"I'm feeling a lot better," she said tentatively.

His fingers tangled in her hair. "Good." His mouth was inches from hers. She could feel the rhythm of his breathing. "Good."

This time it wasn't a getting-to-know-you kiss. They'd covered that in detail last night. This was *I loved what we did before. I want more. I'm taking more.*

Sasha clutched at his shoulders, trying to get closer and closer still. She wanted the weight of him over her, anchoring her to the mattress. But although he deepened the kiss, his tongue stroking the interior of her mouth, he held back.

Begging wasn't something she'd ever done before, but she was ready to start. Except he pulled away to kiss her cheekbone, her brow, then trailed a sparking path down her neck. She shuddered with every touch.

"I can't," he muttered into her collarbone. "God knows I want to strip you bare and lay you back on this mattress—"

"Yes. Let's do that."

She felt his lips curve into a smile against her skin. "You almost died yesterday. I have to be careful with you." He raised his head and framed her face with his hands. "And I still have chores to finish."

Right. She forced herself to breathe slowly, willed her heart to calm down. This wasn't like her, to go right into this kind of intimacy with a guy. She was a slow-burn kind of person. Except everything in this bubble of theirs heightened to the ultimate level. She'd almost touched death yesterday and then awoken to his tender care. Why shouldn't she touch him today? When was she going to get another chance like this?

Stiffly he rose, turning away from her, but not before she saw the bulge in his jeans. He wasn't lying about wanting her. "It should start clearing up tomorrow," he said, his tone strained. "Last night wasn't as cold, and the snow's already started to melt."

It was like a blast of freezing air to her brain. This would all end very soon. In a day or two they'd both be able to leave and get back to their lives. Nothing would be connecting them once she got into her car—assuming it would run—and headed off to her Christmas with Pippa. The Christmas she was meant to have.

No, she wouldn't let herself be sad about that before it even happened. Tomorrow was Christmas, and she was determined to make it special for the both of them.

"That will make it easier to collect greenery," she told Max brightly. Honestly, she was looking forward to whatever they managed to pull together. Even if the decorations were only pine boughs and the feast only the bread he could bake, it would be more than enough.

"Let me finish the chores, and we can get started on the Christmas stuff." When he turned toward her, his body looked more relaxed, sadly. Still deliciously hard and muscled though.

"Can I come? I want to meet Petunia."

"Sure. Let's find you some warmer clothes."

It turned out that Max's clothes didn't fit her very well. She stepped outside, wearing heavy work pants that were tied with baling string and in a coat that swallowed her whole. She had to look ridiculous, but at least she was warm.

Max was watching her with warmth in his eyes. Like he

61

didn't care how she looked, he was just happy to have her there.

"Watch out," he murmured as she almost stepped into a hole hidden by the snow. He cupped her elbow to help her over it, then kept his hand there. So chivalrous.

When they got to the barn, he introduced her to all his horses as he checked their water buckets and gave them grain. He had a funny story about each of them, lots of insights into their individual personalities, and time to give them all some affection.

As she watched Max with his horses, she realized how much he loved them. And she understood why he'd been so short with her when she'd first woken up—he'd been worried about them and Petunia. So worried he hadn't been able to be soft with her.

But then things had calmed down, and she'd seen his gentle side.

"Can I give them some treats?" she asked.

He looked very pleased that she'd asked. "Yeah, there's a big bag of carrots in the feed room. You can grab a handful of those."

Sasha didn't have any experience with horses, not even pony rides as a kid. So it was a dream come true to be able to feed carrots to Max's horses. He showed her how to give the carrots to them, his fingers cupping hers. He stood closer than necessary to her, his thighs and pelvis brushing against her bottom.

She couldn't tell if her heart was racing because she was so close to the horses or because Max was so close to her. Probably a little of both.

Too soon, she'd given out all the carrots, and Max went back to chores. It was amazing—and exhausting—how much work went into the horses. And Max wasn't even riding them today. There was feed to be measured out, stalls to clean, the horses had to be groomed, their feet cleaned, their blankets checked.

Max was totally patient as he did everything though, taking the time and care required without once looking like he'd rather be doing something else. He was completely devoted to his horses, and that touched Sasha. There was nothing like a man who loved animals, and Max clearly loved his.

In fact, his life might even revolve around them. Maybe he didn't have anyone in his life not because he hadn't found her yet but because he didn't have time for a relationship. After all, he had a big family—he didn't have to be alone if he didn't want to be. So maybe he did want to.

That made Sasha's heart sink. He'd chosen a very isolated place to live with no proper house and no cell service, but he seemed content with his life. Did he even want to make room for someone else?

"What's wrong?"

Max's question cut through her dark thoughts. The hose he was filling up the water bucket with kept going, but all his attention was on her. He was good at that, at making her feel like she was the center of everything.

"I'm fine." She forced her future worries to go away. It was Christmas Eve after all, and she was snowed in with a cowboy. "I'm surprised the hose didn't freeze."

"I wrapped everything before the storm came in." He shut off the spigot with a few firm twists of his wrist. "The barn is protected enough that nothing in here froze. But there's a bunch of pipes outside I'm going to have to fix when it thaws. It's going to be a hell of a mess."

Sasha was beginning to suspect she might be a bit of a

mess herself once it thawed and she had to leave. "I'm almost afraid to see what my car looks like."

"I'll go out tomorrow and take a look," Max promised. "With the roads blocked, I'm sure no one's touched it." He gestured for her to follow him to another part of the barn.

Sasha heard the cows before she saw them. She bit her lip in anticipation. "Are they here?"

Max nodded, a smile playing on his mouth. "This here is Mopsy." He looked inside a stall. "She's my other milk cow."

Sasha said hello to the gentle-looking cow, who merely blinked back at her. "She looks so cozy. It's actually pretty warm in here. Oh! She has a baby too."

The calf, who had been lying behind her mom, hauled herself to her feet to get a better look at Sasha. The baby wouldn't come close, but she watched Sasha with open curiosity. The calf was bigger than Poinsettia and seemed more wary. Sasha got the sense she'd never be able to pet this one.

"When was she born?" Sasha asked. "And what's her name?"

"About two months ago. And she doesn't have a name."

Sasha gave him a dirty look. "Max! Everyone else in this barn has a name."

"The Angus cattle don't have names."

Those were the smaller cows he trained his horses on. He hadn't taken her to see them, but she'd caught a whiff of them while she'd been watching him do chores, and that had been enough for her.

"Yes, but you already said you don't keep those. These cows are different."

The little calf swung her head as if in agreement.

"She needs a name," Sasha declared. "That's not fair. Poor thing."

"Maybe she was waiting for you to give her one. You gave Poinsettia a perfect name."

The calf wagged her big spoon ears at that.

Sasha realized that if Max was keeping Poinsettia's name and she ended up naming this calf too some part of her would remain on the ranch even after she left. Max would always have something to remember her by. At least something good and not only his probably awful memories of digging her out of the snow.

"Okay." She rubbed her hands together, the better to get her naming juices flowing. "It should be holiday themed to go with Poinsettia, but not Christmas-holiday themed because that would be too matchy-matchy, don't you think?"

"Of course," Max said gravely. "Maybe Turkey?"

She sent him another dirty look. "A cow named Turkey? That makes no sense. Birds don't even make milk."

"So it has to be milk related too?"

"No, it has to make sense, and Turkey doesn't." Although yesterday was the very first time she'd ever named a cow, she sensed there were rules to it, rules she instinctively knew. She was surprised Max didn't. But thank goodness he hadn't named the calves before she got here, or they might have been stuck with something truly awful. Someone else must have named Petunia and Mopsy.

Sasha tapped her chin. Thanksgiving was close but also didn't suggest very good names. Besides Turkey, which definitely wasn't happening, there wasn't much else that said "adorable calf" in that holiday. Except for... "What do you think about Pumpkin Pie?"

The calf was a delightful shade of reddish brown that

actually reminded her of pumpkin pie. And it rolled off the tongue—it would be awesome to call in Pumpkin Pie every night for milking.

"Oh!" Sasha didn't even let Max answer that. "Do you need to milk them? Can *I* milk them?"

Sometimes guys were annoyed by how she flew off on odd tangents. *Can't you focus even for a second? You can read those books for hours, just pay attention!* More than one guy had said something like that to her when she wasn't sufficiently focused on the conversation. But her mind liked to dart off on tangents, fantasies, and sometimes hop over into new subjects entirely. She couldn't really make herself stop, not that she wanted to.

Max only smiled. "Pumpkin Pie works even though I don't actually like it. The pie, that is, not the name."

"Really? I love it. It's my favorite part of Thanksgiving. I don't know why we can't get pumpkin pie all year round. And I love pumpkin spice too, but it's not quite the same as real pumpkin pie."

"I just like pecan better," he said simply.

She shuddered. "Ew. Pies should not have nuts. Fruit goes in pies, and that's it."

"What about pot pies?"

She waved a hand. "Entirely different category of pie. Like, even though it's called pie, it's not the same thing as dessert pie. Hi, Pumpkin Pie," she said to the calf, who was very interested in their conversation. Maybe the little thing was hoping to try some pumpkin pie one day.

"I'll milk tonight," Max said, "and you can come help."

She couldn't help clapping her hands in delight. She'd gotten to name *two* baby cows, and now she was going to milk too. "This is turning out to be the best Christmas," she said without thinking. When she realized what she'd said, she glanced shyly at Max. "You really don't mind that I'm flighty, do you?"

His expression was soft. "I wouldn't call you flighty. Your mind just works fast. I like it."

A flush climbed up her neck and face. She'd never in her life blushed at a compliment, but that was a pretty good one. Lord, her face was so hot she must be bright pink.

"And yeah, this is a good Christmas," Max said. "Want to go see Petunia and Poinsettia? And then we can gather greenery?"

She nodded, not trusting herself to speak. Could her throat blush? Because it felt like it.

By the time they reached Petunia's stall, Sasha's skin was feeling cooler. And the sight of the big cow with the calf tucked next to her made her exclaim with delight.

"She's up! She's all better."

"She's mending," Max said. "I still need to keep a close eye on her, but things are improving."

Poinsettia came running up, tossing her head and kicking out her front legs. Sasha gave her scratches and rubs as a hello.

"You remember me," she said wonderingly. She'd made friends with a calf. How marvelous.

"She loves you." Max was watching the calf as he said it, but it sent heat rolling through Sasha. A strange kind that made her heart do funny things.

He was talking about the calf, not himself. People didn't fall in love in under twenty-four hours. No matter how much forced proximity and rescuing and only one bed they had thrown at them. And Christmas and being snowed in together, couldn't forget that.

"I love her too," Sasha said softly, making sure to only look at the calf as she said it. Still, her heart did a somersault. It felt exactly like when she read the most emotional moments in her books, when the characters were turning inside out thanks to love, even if they didn't realize it.

Confusion swamped her. Could she really be falling for Max? But what if it was just the fantasy of all this she was responding to: the rescue, the woodstove, the cows?

Sasha knew she could lose herself in her fantasies. Like when she'd crashed the car.

How would her feelings change once the snow melted? And did he even feel the same?

"Let's get started on Christmas," Max said, sounding perfectly normal and not at all in love. "Greenery first, then we'll ransack the freezer for a feast."

Sasha nodded, then made herself speak. "Sounds good. I can wait here if there're more chores to do."

She was going to be fine and normal and remember that it was Christmas Eve and not be sad about anything. Or worried.

As for falling in love... Well, she wouldn't think about that either.

"And that was the year we had a Charlie Brown tree," Sasha finished, telling Max all about her Christmas two years ago with Pippa. "It looked a lot like this branch." She held up a pine branch that was thin and spindly and bent over like it was praying for death.

He was laughing. "How did you get it to stay up? Did you put lights on it?"

"Oh yeah. I had these little fairy lights I got from a tree from the grocery store. And we used stickers as ornaments. We put it in a flower vase and put some of our gifts around it." Sasha smiled wistfully as she remembered. "That was actually a pretty good Christmas even if it was just us."

She caught Max watching her, a smile on his mouth and heat in his eyes. They were gathering pine boughs together, tramping through the snow. Sasha would point out one she liked, and Max would snip it off for her and gather it up.

They both smelled of pine, and their cheeks were flushed with the cold. But Max was right—the freeze was breaking up. It wasn't quite as cold out as it had been, and already the snow was melting in small patches. She didn't want to think about it too much because no snow meant she would have to leave.

Judging by how Max kept looking at her, he didn't want her to leave either. At least not before they shared his bed.

"It sounds fun," he said huskily. He looked down at the pile of branches in his arms. "Think we have enough?"

She wasn't quite ready to quit—it was nice being out here in the weak sunshine with him, tromping through the snow, talking about Christmases past. He hadn't been exaggerating when he said he came from a big family. And apparently they celebrated Christmas for like a month. It sounded... It sounded amazing. And made her a bit homesick.

She considered the pile in his arms and the rest they'd stacked in the back of the side-by-side—she'd learned what the utility vehicle was called today. "I think that's enough." After all, they really only had one room to decorate. "I do wish we had some holly. Or some mistletoe."

The heat in his eyes flared. "I think we can manage without."

Sasha swallowed hard, all of her buzzing. She bet they could.

To cool off and keep herself from dragging him back to

the house, she scooped up some snow. It was tough to move her fingers in the thick gloves Max had given her, but she managed to mash the snow into something like a ball. Or maybe more like a puffy pancake. It was trying to be spherical but wasn't quite getting there.

"Have you ever made snowballs before?" she asked Max as he loaded up the side-by-side.

He shook his head. "I've been sledding up in Pine Ridge but never made snowballs. I don't know why not."

"Me either." She packed another handful of snow onto her half-made snowball. That was something closer to what she imagined a snowball should look like.

And then she cocked her arm and sent the snowball sailing into Max's back.

It didn't burst, not really. She had a terrible throwing arm, so it mostly bounced off him and landed at his feet. It wasn't anything like it was supposed to be, exploding into a cloud of snowflakes, Max yelping as it hit.

He went very still instead. Dangerously still.

Sasha stiffened. Oh no, maybe that had been the wrong move. Maybe he was mad now and not charmed by her starting a snowball fight.

That was the problem with all the fantasies she spun up. She expected people to react like they were in books—to jump right in when she threw a snowball at them—and they didn't realize.

He turned so slowly her heart stopped. But when she saw his face and the grin there, happy adrenaline kicked through her.

"You're in trouble now." He reached down to scoop up two handfuls of snow.

Sasha was laughing even as she started running. She ducked behind one of the trees, breathing fast, mouth aching from her smile. She gathered snow as quickly as she could, pressing it into some kind of shape. It looked even worse than her first effort, but at least it was holding together. That was all it needed to do until it hit Max.

She peeped around the tree trunk. Immediately snow exploded across her chest. She hadn't even seen him throw that.

Of course, he hadn't seen her throw either, but that was because she'd been sneaky. He was just plain fast. And accurate.

She ducked back behind the tree, considered her strategy. She was going to have to get sneaky again.

"There's no way you haven't done this before," she called. "You've practiced."

His laugh rang out. "Nope. I'm just naturally this good."

Ooh, the note of pride in his voice played on her nerves in the best way. Normally humbleness was attractive to her, but his confidence had its appeal too.

"Come on out," he cajoled. "You started this."

"I'm being strategic."

"Strategic?" he asked. "Or scared?"

She laughed at that. "I'm not falling for it. You want me to get all huffy and come blazing out and you'll tag me again." She poked her head out the barest amount. "Hey! You're taking shelter too!"

He was, crouching next to the side-by-side with a pile of snowballs next to him. "All's fair in love and war, baby."

Something inside her sparked and crackled. *Love. Baby.* She was having a snowball fight with a man who'd rescued her, who'd cuddled her all through the night. Who loved his animals and had a core of nobility that ran bone-deep. It was almost too much.

So she jumped out from behind the tree and started

throwing wildly, tossing snowballs as fast as she formed them, running straight for Max.

Every one of her snowballs missed, but she didn't slow down. He tossed a few himself, but she didn't feel them hit.

She was laughing as he caught her, the two of them going down into the snow. Max flipped them so that he was beneath her. Their breaths came out in puffs as they laughed together.

And then they were kissing. Max was solid and warm and strong beneath her, and his mouth was hungry, needy. But he was still smiling somehow too. So was she.

"You okay?" he asked as he smoothed her hair behind her ear.

"Great," Sasha said. "I've never had a snowball fight before."

"What was that berserker attack there at the end?"

"It worked, didn't it?" she asked smugly. "Look at where we are." She leaned a little more into him, reminding him he was under her.

His gaze darkened. "Is this where I'm supposed to surrender?" He held up one hand. "Okay, I give up. Use me however you want."

Now there was an invitation she couldn't resist. She licked her lips and studied him. However she wanted was going to be a tall order. It would probably take hours, weeks, months.

She leaned down and licked his lower lip. There was a hint of salt there, and coffee. The stubble at the boundary of his mouth roughed over her tongue.

He groaned. So she took his lower lip between her own, squeezing gently. The rasp of his stubble was so much sharper against her lips. His mouth was soft though, slick. She ran her teeth over the skin, savoring his gasp.

Her hands fisted in his jacket, the gloves making it difficult. Too many clothes. But there was also something hotly sweet about it all, kissing him in the snow with so many layers between them. All they could do was kiss, which made it that much more intense.

She licked at one corner of his mouth, inhaled the scent of his skin. She nuzzled along the underside of his jaw, and he released a noise that sounded like a strangled laugh. So he was ticklish there then.

Running her teeth over his Adam's apple made him grunt. One of his hands landed on her hip and squeezed. She clenched inside at the hard pressure of his fingers. Her pulse kicked up its heels.

She braced herself on his wide shoulders and kissed him deeply, tongues tangling together. She was hungry, so desperate, and he met her need for need. Her heart beat hard throughout her, especially at her core. All of her sizzled, sparked, even the touch of her clothes against her skin almost too much.

"Sasha." Max said her name like she'd always dreamed someone would, a splintered moan of need that only she could answer. "Sasha. God, you're so hot. I can't believe you."

He made her sound like a dream come true. A wicked dream of twisted sheets and sweat-sheened skin. She might even be sweating now under all her layers—the urge to tear them off and let the air and him kiss her bare skin was almost unbearable.

He shifted so that her legs spread, making room for him between her thighs. Her knees sank into the snow, cold and damp, but she didn't care because she was hot and wet where their bodies met. He thrust against her, the motion so sharp and graceless it felt almost like he didn't know he was doing it. That his desire had completely taken over.

She rolled her hips into that pressure, felt the hard length of him. Her eyes went wide. If she could feel *that* through all those layers, then he was pretty impressive.

She was panting, her mouth was raw from the kisses, and the rest of her positively ached. Oh, and her knees were starting to go numb from the snow, not that she could care that much.

"Sweetheart." Max's voice was strained as he ran his gloved hand along her jaw. "Honey. I want this, God, do I want you, but... not in the snow. I just dug you out of this..."

Right. Right, she'd narrowly escaped death just yesterday. But she felt so alive... She squeezed her thighs, feeling sensation arc through her core, spark through her most sensitive spot. She closed her eyes, tried to remember that she had a brain and could use it. But even her brain yelped in protest at the thought of releasing Max.

There's a bed back at the house. Just one bed.

"I feel fine," she said even as she got up. She held out a hand to him.

He gave her a look that said, *Are you kidding?* before jumping to his feet in one fluid movement. "I'd pull you over," he said gruffly as he gently brushed snow off her. He gave himself a much rougher dust off.

"I'm tougher than you think," she said as she watched him.

His gaze was hot when it met hers. "I know you're tough. You survived—and bounced back from—something that might have killed you. I'm awed by how tough you are."

Her mouth dropped open. Never in a million years would Sasha have considered herself tough. A romantic, yes. A daydreamer, of course.

Tough? No. Not Sasha, who had a marshmallow in place of her heart.

That marshmallow was melting like it was about to be smooshed into a s'more. A s'more made up of her marshmallow heart and his dark, chocolaty kisses. With a helping of his graham-cracker-sweet secret heart.

No one had ever called her tough. And she'd have never known how much that would touch her if Max hadn't done it.

He gave her a quick, firm kiss. "Come on, tough girl. Let's go raid the freezers for dinner."

She caught up his hand and pressed herself into his side. He immediately hooked an arm over her shoulder. It felt right, like they'd been doing this forever. Like they'd keep doing it for decades to come.

Except they wouldn't. This was a one-day, maybe two-day-long interlude. When the snow melted, it would end.

She snuggled closer to Max, seeking his warmth. And not letting herself think of tomorrow.

6

"I can't believe I forgot about these tamales," Max said as he rigged up a steamer on the stove. Usually he microwaved them, which his mother would have said was a crime, but without power, he had to improvise.

And it was Christmas Eve. You couldn't *microwave* tamales for a day as special as that.

Sasha looked up from where she was stringing paper chains along the walls. "It's amazing what you have in that freezer. Tamales, pies, veggies—we're going to have a feast tonight."

"Well, they are almost a year old, so they might be a bit freezer burned," he warned.

His mom had packed them up for him last Christmas, and he'd put them to the back of the freezer, intending to get them out one night when he was feeling like tamales. Except they'd had some frozen pork chops put on top of them, then a bag of fries, and eventually he'd forgotten they were there. It had been like striking gold to find them.

It wasn't really Christmas without tamales. While he appreciated everything Sasha was doing with the decorations, honestly, he would have felt the holiday was entirely complete with just the tamales.

"I'm sure they'll still be delicious." She stepped back and studied her work. "I don't know. I really wish I had at least one strand of sparkle lights."

He put the lid on the pot and went over to kiss her temple. "It looks great. All of it." He wrapped his arms around her, and she leaned back into him.

God, it felt so right to hold her like this. It also felt right to kiss her in the snow. And spoon her as he slept.

Every way he touched her felt right. It made him think... Well, it made him *feel* he was falling for her. Already had maybe.

Max had never thought much about love. Sure, his parents were happy, and he had a massive family—he was surrounded by that kind of love. Which was probably why he hadn't thought about settling down yet.

And then Sasha fell into his life, and it was like something inside him had opened. Some door he didn't even know was closed, but now light and life flooded through.

He couldn't say anything though. She might talk about instalove in her romance novels—she'd explained to him at length about her favorite books while they gathered the pine boughs—but how was that supposed to even work in real life? She might not even feel the same way.

No, better to keep it to himself and simply enjoy the time he had with her. She was certainly attracted to him—God, he'd been about to strip her bare right there in the snow before his better sense intervened.

There was a difference between sex and love, and he'd had enough of the former to know it. With Sasha, it was different. At least for him.

He wondered if she'd ever know that she was giving him

the most memorable Christmas ever. Yes, he missed his family, but being here with her was more than enough.

"I guess it does look nice," she said as her head rested on his chest.

"More than nice," he said into her hair. She smelled of her flowery shampoo still. "You made it into a real holiday."

"We both did." She ran her hand along his forearm. It felt like something a girlfriend would do.

"The tamales will be a while," he said. "What do you want to do while we wait?"

Max held his breath while he waited for her answer. He'd put the mattress back on his bed, and while the room was cold, they'd be warm enough under the blankets. If she wanted to pass time the same way he was thinking.

The movement of her hand on his forearm slowed, became more intent. His heart thudded hard in his ears.

"You moved the mattress," she said softly.

There was no mistaking that. Or the way she was caressing him, leaning into him. He brushed his mouth over her temple.

"Yes." His voice was gravelly.

"Will we be warm enough in the bedroom?" The heat in her tone made the question pointless.

"You know we will."

She twisted to lift her face to his. Their mouths met in a rush of need. She turned in his arms, and in the same moment, he lifted her. She wrapped her legs around him, and he bit back a groan. She fit too perfectly against him, her hungry mouth and hands igniting his own need.

He wasn't going to be able to let her go when the time came. He'd have to, but he already knew it would break his heart.

But he had her for now, and he wasn't going to waste a moment on future regrets.

He marched them into the bedroom, carefully laying her down on the blanket she'd brought. It smelled like her shampoo, like flowers on the first day of summer.

She was still wearing the warm clothes he'd given her, her shapely curves hidden beneath all that fabric. But he knew they were there—she'd just now pressed them against him and again last night, when she'd curled up in his arms.

It was cold in the room even though the day had warmed up. He'd have to be careful undressing her so that she didn't get cold.

Which gave him a great idea.

"Get under the covers. Leave your clothes on," he said to her when she reached for the hem of her shirt.

Her mouth dropped open. "I wasn't suggesting we take a nap. In case I wasn't clear when I..." She gestured to his arm, his mouth, then all of him.

He couldn't help his laugh. "No, honey, that came through loud and clear." He leaned in and nipped her bottom lip. "Trust me, we're on the same page. Get under the covers. You'll like it, I promise."

"Mmm." Sasha cocked one eyebrow, looking so sexy and sassy he almost let her get her way. "If you promise."

He helped her under the covers, tucking the blanket that had saved her life tightly around her. "Warm enough?" Max asked, and as he did, he realized he'd probably always worry about that. Once she was gone and he thought of her, he'd immediately wonder if she was warm enough.

If she stayed with him, he'd make sure of that always. But he had to let her go.

"I'm toasty." She wriggled her toes under the blankets. "Honestly, it's amazing how warm this blanket is. Pippa gave it to me. I think her great-aunt made it." Her gaze flicked to his. "This is your big plan? To tuck me in?"

He kissed her again, just to show her that no, that wasn't his plan. "Be patient."

When he started pulling off his clothes, her eyes went wide. "No fair," she said huskily. "You're getting naked, and I'm stuck here with all my clothes on."

When his shirt hit the floor, her mouth made the most adorable O. He felt strong as an ox when she looked at him like that, like he could move an entire mountain of snow or more for her.

"Okay." She licked her lips. "I'm getting convinced."

He smiled as he reached for the button on his jeans. "Should I try harder?"

She giggled and rolled her eyes at his dumb joke. "Yes. You definitely should."

Max made himself go slow, to give her a proper show. He'd never done this with anyone before, never even thought about it, but he knew Sasha liked fantasies. He wanted to make one happen for her.

So he was stripping in front of her while she watched him with devouring eyes. He had to admit it was hot as hell. Peeling each inch of fabric back, giving her another bit of his body, while she took it all in. He was hard as a rock and already lightly sweating.

His boxers fell to the floor.

Sasha gasped. "Wow," she mouthed.

Somehow the fact that she couldn't even say it out loud made him want to laugh and combust with need at the same time. How did she manage to do that with one little unspoken word?

Because she was amazing and remarkable and beautiful. That was why.

"When do I get to look with my fingers?" she said breathlessly. "Because my eyes can't take much more."

Okay, maybe he had some fantasies of his own he'd never known about, because that right there fulfilled a bunch of them.

"Show's not over," he told her with a wink. As much as he wanted to climb in with her, bare skin against bare skin, he was enjoying this too.

To make her laugh again, he flexed like a muscleman, showing off his arms, his chest, his thighs, even his butt. She made a strangled noise that might have been a laugh or a moan when he did that.

She was panting when he turned around. The naked need in her expression undid him—there was no way he could resist her.

"Please," Sasha said, her voice breaking, but he was already slipping into the bed, pulling her close to him.

She came eagerly, her limbs wrapping around his. They kissed for long moments, stealing desperate gasps of air whenever they forced themselves to stop.

"I loved your show," Sasha said as she kissed her way along his jaw. Her teeth scraped his earlobe, and he shuddered at the sensation. "A brilliant, big plan."

He tried to gather up his thoughts, but they scattered under her mouth. "That wasn't my plan." He reached for the hem of her T-shirt, rubbing the fabric between his thumb and finger. "I had something else in mind."

"What?" She lifted her head and blinked at him. "There was something else?"

"Yes." He shifted so that she was beneath him, her delicious body still covered by clothes—and by his naked one. "Let me show you."

7

Sasha never would have guessed Max was such a showman.

A striptease? And a *muscle* show-off? Maybe she had died out there in the snow and this was all some elaborate dream, because it was *heavenly*.

He made her laugh. He made sure she was warm. He cut pine boughs to make a Christmas celebration.

Max was better than any imagined hero she'd ever thought up. And somehow she would have to leave him.

Sasha would never again doubt instalove stories. Because it was happening to her. Just like that, she was falling for Max.

His fingers twisted into the hem of her shirt, pulling the fabric across her skin. She was so worked up even that sensation made her want to arch off the bed.

She put her hand over his and started pulling. She wanted her clothes off, and she wanted them off now.

But he resisted her, his strength too much for her to overcome.

"What?" she said with naked frustration. "Don't you want me to take my clothes off?"

"No." His voice was so deep, like it was dragging out from the bottom of his throat. "*I* want to do it." He tugged with her hand still over his, encouraging her to let go. "Let me."

So she did. She opened her hand and opened herself to whatever he might do.

What he did do was the most amazing, mind-blowing undressing she'd ever experienced, but all under the covers. "So you stay warm," he'd said softly into her ear as he worked her shirt up inch by inch. "I don't ever want you to be cold again. Never."

No chance of that, not when she was on fire. Every bit of skin he uncovered, he explored, caressed, stroked. He discovered sensitive spots no other person ever had. Or maybe it was all Max, awakening parts of her no one else could have.

He didn't limit himself to his fingers either. He inhaled the crook of her neck, groaning as if her scent—just her scent!—drove him mad. He licked the underside of her breast, and she almost screamed.

The words he whispered into her skin were almost as potent as his touch. *You're so beautiful, I can't believe you're so perfect,* and other endearments along with dirtier, darker words. What he wanted to do to her, how long he'd been wanting her, how she was beyond even his imaginings.

By the time he was reaching for the waistband of her pants, she was already achingly close to the edge, feeling swollen and needy between her legs. If he even just skimmed his hand there, she'd explode.

He loosened the drawstring, then slipped his hands around to her back and under the elastic of her underwear.

He took two full handfuls of her ass and squeezed, grinding her against his hardness.

"Do you feel what you do to me?" he gritted out. Again he thrust against her, and the wet fabric of her panties clung to her folds.

Sasha had never been this aroused before. Even the thrum of her pulse was agonizing under her skin, too much sensation to bear. "Feel what you do to me," she begged, needing his touch there.

He squeezed her ass again, then shook his head as he reluctantly released her. She whimpered, but he held strong.

"No," he said harshly, mostly to himself. "Slow. Slow, I promised to savor *every* inch of you."

"Really," she babbled, feeling like she was about to burst out of her skin, "there's only a few particular inches that need attention. Like, *really* need attention."

He dropped his head into the crook of her neck and started laughing quietly. "Sasha, I have never been so turned on in my life, and you're still making me laugh. How do you even do that?"

The wonder in his tone caught at her heart. And now that piece of her felt overloaded with sensation too. "I don't know," she said helplessly. "I just am the way I am."

"And I'm so grateful for it." When he lifted his head, his gaze burned into her. "Let me show you how much."

This time when he touched her—the slope of her thigh, dip of her knee, arch of her foot, even all of her toes—she felt his hands trembling. Like even those simple touches were too much for him.

Sasha felt both completely vulnerable—after all, she could barely speak she was so worked up—and entirely powerful all at once. She could make this man tremble.

He could make her shudder. So they were evenly matched there. Perfectly matched in fact.

Her panties he saved for last. She helped him with a mighty kick of her legs that lifted the blankets and sent her underwear flying clear across the room.

After that, his restraint finally cracked. His first brush of her folds was slow, light, but then he gave a guttural groan. "You're so wet."

Sasha grabbed his hand, digging her nails into his wrist, and put his fingers right where she wanted them. Who cared if she was being greedy?

Not Max, who kissed her like he wanted to devour her as she rode his hand, racing toward her climax.

When she came undone, her entire body jackknifed, curling in on itself as waves and waves rolled over her. She might have grunted or moaned or God only knew what kind of noises she made—she certainly didn't.

By the time she could unfold herself, Max had already put on a condom and was positioning himself over her. Somehow, miraculously, the blanket was still covering both of them.

"Yes, yes, yes," she hissed as he pressed forward. She was still way too sensitive, and it was going to— "Oh my God."

"I-I just..." Max's expression was strained, his entire body taut as a bowstring. "Do you need a minute?"

"No." She almost shouted it, but the last thing she needed was a minute. She needed him to *move* She rolled her hips to prove her point and gasped at the feel of him stretching her, filling her.

"Are you warm enough?"

She looked straight into his eyes. "I'm burning."

They moved together, so perfectly in tune Sasha was

sure it couldn't be real. This kind of intimacy didn't happen, not outside her fantasies, but it was. It was *real*. So real she could feel her heart cracking open as a second orgasm took her, splitting so wide open there was no hope of repair as Max joined her a few seconds later.

Instead of collapsing on her, he rolled over and gathered her up, kissing her temple between shaking, sharp breaths. Her breathing was just as harsh. But he immediately made her feel... *loved*. There was no other way to describe it.

And somehow the blanket still covered both of them. Like it was magically attached to them, determined to keep them warm.

"I have to go take care of this real quick," Max said after a time. "Are you warm enough?"

Sasha wanted to laugh. She wanted to cry. She wanted to ask him if she could stay forever, under the blanket, a Christmas just for the two of them.

"I'm good," she said, her voice only slightly thin. "Great, actually. Better than great." And she really was, even with her weird, sad reaction to his question.

"Me too." He kissed her again for several long moments. "I really do have to take care of this. And check on the tamales."

Sasha would say she wasn't stopping him, but she really was. And since tonight was likely all she had with him, she kept it up. And didn't let herself regret it one bit.

8

When Sasha woke up, she was alone.

Warm and cozy under the blanket that Pippa had given her, the blanket that had saved her life, and a touch sore from everything they'd done last night, but still alone.

Light, strong and bright, streamed through the window. It felt warm on her cheek.

She sat up. Max must have gone out to feed. And with the sun so high and bright, the sky so clear....

The snow had to be melting.

Even though it was Christmas Day, her heart sank. No more snow meant no more excuse to stay here. Max would want to get back to his life. And she would have to get back to hers.

Please let my car be broken.

An awful thing to pray for, because she couldn't afford any repairs. But... it would give her an excuse to stay longer.

Sasha threw off the covers and went searching for the clothes she'd worn yesterday. It wasn't like her car was even here and running yet. She still had time with Max. And she wanted to go check on Poinsettia and Petunia.

"Oh brr," she yelled as the air hit her bare skin. God, but that was cold. How had they been so warm last night?

She blushed as she remembered, which somehow made the air feel even colder. After their first intense round in bed, they'd eaten the feast of tamales and fresh-cooked bread and an apple pie they'd found in the freezer with the tamales. It had been perhaps the strangest Christmas dinner Sasha had ever had and maybe the best too. The tamales had been excellent, the bread tasty, and she'd had two slices of pie just because.

They'd talked and laughed and kissed and touched as they'd eaten. It was like they'd been intimate for years instead of hours. She'd sang him some of her favorite Christmas carols while he'd looked on adoringly even though she knew her voice was only okay. But she couldn't let Christmas go by without some songs.

Max had refused to sing—"I don't have any favorite songs, and you sing better anyway"—but he had danced with her across the room, humming a song for them.

And then they'd gone back to bed. But not to sleep.

Sasha hurriedly pulled on her clothes, her blush fading. When she went into the main room, she saw that Max had already stoked the fire in the stove—it was toasty warm—and a pot of coffee sat on the stovetop. He'd left out a mug for her too along with some slices of homemade bread.

He really was too perfect. Sasha hoped he never got her car out.

She poured herself a cup, then grabbed some bread before going out to find Max.

And stopped dead right by the door.

Her suitcase. It was sitting in the corner, on the other

side of the little table, so she hadn't seen it at first.

Her heart stopped, then started again, almost too slow. She stared at the boring gray fabric, same as a million other wheeled suitcases.

If it was here, that meant Max had made it out to her car. Maybe he'd even dug it out. If the car was running...

She'd have to leave.

She dashed out the front door. Sure enough, there was her car parked right out front. The right front bumper was crumpled from where she'd landed in the snowbank, but the rest of it looked okay. Dirty, but okay.

Maybe he had to tow it here with the tractor. Maybe it doesn't run.

She'd left the keys inside it in case anyone found it and needed to move it. No one would have bothered to steal it—the car was too old and boring. But she refused to see if the car would start.

She would find Max first. Ask him what had happened. And... She swallowed hard, her eyes already burning.

And tell him goodbye if she had to.

She found him in Petunia's stall, checking on her and Poinsettia. When he saw her, his face lit up so brightly it hurt to see.

"You're awake." He took a step toward her, then stopped when he caught her expression. "Everything okay?"

She was supposed to be happy. He'd gotten her car for her. She could go on with her life just like she'd planned. Crying and throwing a fit was no way to repay him.

"You found my car." She forced herself to smile. "You must have been up early this morning."

"Yeah, it wasn't very far from where I found you." He tilted his head as he studied her. "Are you sure you're okay?"

"I'm so glad you found the car." Her tone was brittlely bright. "I don't know how I'll ever repay you. Does it... does it run?"

She wanted to shout *no* when he nodded. "I drove it back here just fine." His expression, everything about him, was slowly closing off, inch by inch. "You could head out to your friend's now. The roads were clear when I went out."

He sounded like he had when she'd first woken up. Distant. Stiff.

She knew he wasn't anything like that, which made it hurt all the worse.

"You can get to your Christmas too," she said. "With your family. Now that Petunia is all better."

"Yeah." He lifted his hand, then let it fall against his thigh. The gesture looked almost hopeless. "You should really see a doctor. Just in case."

She didn't want to tell him she didn't really have a doctor since her deductible was so high. If something was really wrong, she'd just go to urgent care, not that she had yet. He'd probably insist she see someone, make the appointment himself, drive her too, and that would be too...

She tried to swallow down her agony and almost choked on it. "I feel fine now," she said. "But I'll make an appointment as soon as I get home."

His brow creased. The genuine concern on his face... It was too much. He looked ready to march her to the doctor himself.

She sucked in a breath. "Anyway, I'll let you get back to it. Thank you for everything." She made herself march to the stall door before she could do anything stupid. "Merry Christmas."

Poinsettia bawled. Long and low and terribly sad.

A tear slipped down Sasha's cheek. She hadn't properly

said goodbye to the baby or to Pumpkin Pie, but if she turned back now, she'd completely break down.

But even as she told herself it was better this way, to just make a clean break and be done with it, she knew she was lying. It still hurt. It hurt like hell.

"Sasha." He said her name with deep command and even deeper emotion.

She stopped dead but didn't turn around. She had to preserve some bit of poise, and if she totally lost it... "What?" she asked in a splintered tone.

Had she forgotten something? If so, she was fine just leaving it. She only wanted to run away from him and this pain. But of course the pain would follow her.

"I don't want you to go." He said it so matter-of-factly, like it was the truest thing in the world. And like he was as torn in this moment as she was.

That made her turn around. His expression speared her right through. His need for her, how badly he wanted her, was open on his face, not even a bit hidden.

He had more courage than she did, not putting a brave face on this parting. He'd just... come out and said it.

"I know it seems crazy," he went on. "We only just met each other. But that doesn't make my feelings for you any less real." His voice deepened. "And they are real."

Sasha couldn't speak. There was too much caught up inside her—hope, disbelief, and pure happiness. Somehow it all combined to make her cry even harder.

"It happened the moment I saw you in the snow," he said. "It just hit me and I knew—you're the one. The one I've been waiting for." He gave her a small smile. "Well, my heart knew. It took my brain a minute to figure it out." He gestured to the cows watching him. "I had kind of a lot going on."

Sasha could only laugh through her tears. There was way too much going on inside her to speak, so she simply launched herself at him.

Max caught her perfectly, his strong arms enclosing her. She wrapped her legs around his waist, feeling like she'd come home.

"I thought I was crazy too," she babbled between kisses. "That I feel this way after so short a time. I mean, has it even been twenty-four hours? But I wanted to die, having to leave you. Maybe I just read too many books—"

"You don't read too many books. I love how much you love them."

"—I mean, this doesn't happen to anyone. That they meet in a snowstorm and just... fall in love."

She framed his face with her hands as he studied her with a soft, fond expression. How could she have ever thought she could walk away from him?

"It happened to us," he said with deep resolve. "We're living proof that it can happen." He freed one hand to snap his fingers. "Just like that."

It felt like a miracle. Sasha's heart seemed to open and open and open some more, expanding to fit all her feelings in it. And even then, it seemed too tight, like there was even more growing it needed to do. After all, they'd only just fallen in love. They had a lot more love to build together.

Except... "How will it work?" she asked. "You're up here. I'm down in Brawley."

He shrugged. "We'll figure it out. We'll be together on the weekends. I do take those off. Can you work from home?"

She nodded. "I already am."

"Then I'll put in satellite internet. And get the house finished."

Yes, she wanted to move in here. To always be with him. Although that was a bit fast.

Or was it? She'd never felt like this about anyone. Maybe she never would again.

Maybe she needed to grab this happiness.

"I know it's a lot," Max said, reading her expression. "But I've never asked anyone to live with me before. And it's going to take some time to finish the house." His brows drew together. "In case you decide to change your mind."

He looked so vulnerable it almost broke her heart.

"I won't," she said, and she knew it was true. Maybe it was fast, but it felt right. More right than anything else in her life. "And you're right—we'll make it work."

Max kissed her then, his relief and happiness flowing through her. They stayed that way for a long time. Sasha knew she'd never been so content in her entire life.

This was where she was meant to be. Thank goodness she'd slammed into that snowbank, or she never would have found him.

Something butted into her leg. Hard and insistent.

She looked down to see Poinsettia rubbing her poll against Sasha's thigh. *Give me some attention too!* the little calf seemed to be saying.

Max let her slide down his body, still holding her close. "That calf loves you."

Sasha rubbed Poinsettia's head. "I love her too. Sweet baby." She looked back up at Max, her whole world in his eyes. "And I love you too."

He smiled as he leaned in for another kiss. "I think you might love the calf more. But that's okay. She's cuter than me."

Sasha was still laughing when their mouths met.

9

"Wait, he just rode up out of the snow? Just in time to rescue you?" The expression on Pippa's face was so flabbergasted Sasha had to laugh.

"Yeah," she said with a fond glance at Max, "he did. It was perfect timing. But then, he's pretty much perfect."

They'd come up to Cabrillo to spend Christmas with Pippa and her boyfriend Bear at his house. Pippa was living in a travel trailer while her house was being rebuilt, and it turned out that a trailer wasn't a great place to ride out a freak blizzard. So they'd gathered in the Westfall family ranch house to eat a prime rib roast, scalloped potatoes, green bean casserole, and a homemade apple pie.

Sasha had privately thought that as good as it all was, it wasn't as delicious as the tamales they'd had last night.

Sasha had asked if Max wanted to head to his family's place for Christmas, but the roads down the hill were still snowed in. So they'd go visit them tomorrow. Sasha was only slightly terrified at the thought of meeting his entire family, but Max assured her they'd all love her. He'd called his mom to tell her everything that had happened during the snowstorm, and she was already begging to meet the woman her son had fallen for.

Sasha's family was less enthusiastic, but they were glad she was okay. "You only just met him," her mom had said when Sasha had detailed everything. "Are you sure?"

"More than anything," Sasha had said. "You'll understand when you meet him."

Pippa sighed wistfully. "Wow. So you found a cowboy too. Was it like something out of a book when he rode up?"

"Well, I was kind of passed out," Sasha said. "So I missed most of it. And I woke up next to the calf."

"Ah yeah," Pippa said carelessly, "Bear's always got calves he's raising in the bummer barn."

It seemed her friend was already well adjusted to ranch life. Sasha supposed she'd be the same way in a few months: just totally okay with giving baby cows bottles in the kitchen.

Across the room, Max caught her eye. He was talking to Bear and Sayer about something, probably horses. It turned out that they already knew each other, which made sense. Cabrillo wasn't a big town, and they all had ranches.

"It's a beautiful story," Pippa said, "and if he's friends with Bear, he must be a good dude, but... are you sure? It's very fast, and you went through a lot."

Sasha held Max's gaze. Her heart sped up, excitement running through her, all prickly and electric. But she also felt safe.

"I'm sure," she said simply. "When you knew with Bear... Well, I just did the same with Max, only quicker."

Pippa looked over to Bear and smiled to herself. "It took us longer because we had some things to tussle over. He can be so pigheaded." She said it like it was the best thing in the world about him.

Sasha was very glad Max wasn't pigheaded. Instead, he was kind and strong and so brave. And he loved his animals.

"Do you remember that blanket you gave me?" she asked Pippa.

Pippa's brow scrunched up. "The crocheted one? I think so. It was pink, right?"

"Purple," Sasha said. It was spread over Max's bed right now, waiting for them. "It saved my life, you know. I took it with me when I left the car, trying to keep warm. And Max saw it poking out of the snow, which is how he even knew I was there. If it hadn't been..."

Pippa shivered. "Oh my God. You could have died."

"But the blanket kept me warm until Max found me."

Pippa chewed on her lip. "I don't remember that blanket being that thick. It was like something you'd find on a sofa."

"It's not heavy at all. But it's incredibly warm." Sasha remembered how it had kept her and Max toasty all last night in his unheated bedroom. She hadn't felt even a bit of chill.

Pippa stared at her oddly. "Like... *magically* warm?"

Sasha stared back for a moment. "You said that the packages left on your front porch, the ones you couldn't figure out where they were from—that was Bear. Right? That was him?"

"Yeah," Pippa said slowly. "It was all him. No magic."

A shudder moved through Sasha because Pippa didn't sound very certain. But if the blanket was enchanted, it was a good enchantment. It had literally saved her life.

"No magic," Sasha said in a strained voice, trying to convince herself.

Pippa gave herself a shake. "The more important thing is, if you're with Max, that means I'll see you so much more often! You'll be up here all the time."

"We can double date," Sasha squealed. That had always been a fantasy of hers, not that she wanted to do it while Pippa had been dating James, who was a lazy jerk. Bear was so much better. And he and Max already got along.

It was too perfect. It was all just too perfect. A Christmas to remember always.

Max took that moment to come over to them, giving Pippa a friendly smile and a much hotter look to Sasha.

"Hey," he said to her, holding out his hand. "I want to show you something."

Pippa stifled a laugh. "Sure. You kids go have fun." She sent Sasha an exaggerated wink.

"She's really happy for you," Max said as Pippa went to find Bear. "I like her."

"She likes you too. We're going to double date," Sasha said. "What did you want to show me?"

Max drew her into the entryway of the house, which was hidden from the living room where everyone was gathered by a wall. No one could see them in the shadows back here.

Sasha approved. She'd been desperate to be alone with him or at least touch him for the past fifteen minutes. She'd gone too long without him near.

Already, she was completely addicted.

Max pulled her to his body so that she was cradled between his legs. She breathed in deeply, taking in his clean, warm scent.

"Did you really want to show me something," she whispered huskily, "or was that just an excuse?"

He smiled and pointed to the ceiling above her head. "Look."

She tilted her head back and saw— "Mistletoe!" She only just managed to keep from shouting it. "You found some."

"That's right. Not that I really need the excuse to kiss you. But I'll take it anyway."

And then they had their first kiss under the mistletoe. But Sasha knew it wouldn't be their last.

Epilogue

ne Year Later

Max grabbed Sasha's arm and helped her around a rock in the driveway. "Watch out."

"I can't," she said with an edge to her tone. "You made me put on this blindfold. Remember?"

He smiled to himself. She usually loved surprises, but since he hadn't let her see the house for the past two weeks, she was testy. "I won't let you fall."

"I've seen the entire thing," she reminded him. "And picked out the cabinets, paint, and carpet. It's kind of silly, isn't it?"

"You haven't seen all of it." He guided her up the driveway until she was facing the front porch.

It had taken a year to finish the house, the two of them spending their nights in the little converted shed. Sasha claimed she didn't mind, not when she had internet—she'd moved in with him about two months after that wild, amazing Christmas—but Max had minded. The shed was fine for just him, but he wanted a proper house for the woman he loved.

The work had seemed excruciatingly slow at times, but Max had wanted everything perfect for Sasha. So he'd forced himself to be patient.

But now it was finally ready for them to move in. To begin the rest of their lives.

"Can I take it off now?" she asked.

A low moo from the front lawn had her going still. Max stifled his sigh. Poinsettia was going to ruin the surprise if she didn't keep her mouth shut.

And then Poinsettia started running for Sasha, whom she loved better than anything. Max whipped off the blindfold before Sasha got knocked over.

"Poinsettia!" she called, greeting the calf who wasn't so little anymore. "What are you doing out here?" She caught sight of the house and gasped, her mouth falling open as her eyes went wide. "Oh my goodness. It's so beautiful."

Exactly the reaction Max had been hoping for. He'd been rushing the painters and the landscapers the past two weeks, trying to get the house ready for them to move in before Christmas. They were only five days away now, but the house was finally done.

Poinsettia nudged Sasha's hand.

"What's on your neck?" Sasha asked. "It's a ribbon..."

She caught sight of the box tied to the ribbon and went quiet. Her hands went over her mouth and her gaze flew to Max.

"It's yours," he said. "Your surprise, along with the house. I wanted to wait until it was done."

With trembling fingers, Sasha untied the box from the

ribbon. As she snapped it open, Max went down to one knee.

"I'm already the happiest man in the world," he said. "But would you do me the honor of being my wife? I need you. All of us do." He gestured to Poinsettia. "We all love you so much and want you with us forever."

Poinsettia mooed in approval.

Tears ran down Sasha's cheeks. "It's gorgeous. All of this is so beautiful. The house, the ring, Poinsettia..." She gulped in a breath. "And you." She reached for Max. "You're the best of all. Of course I'll marry you. And we'll have lots of horses and cows and babies together."

She pulled him up to his feet. He took the chance to slip the ring on her finger, where it sparkled gaily. Like a Christmas light.

"Finding you in the snow was the best thing that ever happened to me."

"It was the best thing that ever happened to me too."

They walked together into their new house, right to the bedroom where Max had already made up the bed.

Their favorite blanket was already laid over it and waiting for them.

Thanks for reading *Cowboy, Kiss Me at Christmas*! The next book in the series is *Cowboy, Hold Me Forever*—you can grab it here!

Thanks for reading! Sign up for my newsletter and get free books, exclusive content, and new release news!

About the Author

Genevieve Turner is a *USA Today* bestselling author of western romance. She loves cowboys, the rural life, and happily ever afters. She lives in beautiful Southern California with the perfect number of kids, dogs, and turkeys—and probably too many chickens.

You can find her on the web at www.genturner.com.

Genevieve's Newsletter

NEW RELEASES, SALES, AND A *Free* STARTER LIBRARY WHEN YOU SIGN UP!

CLICK HERE